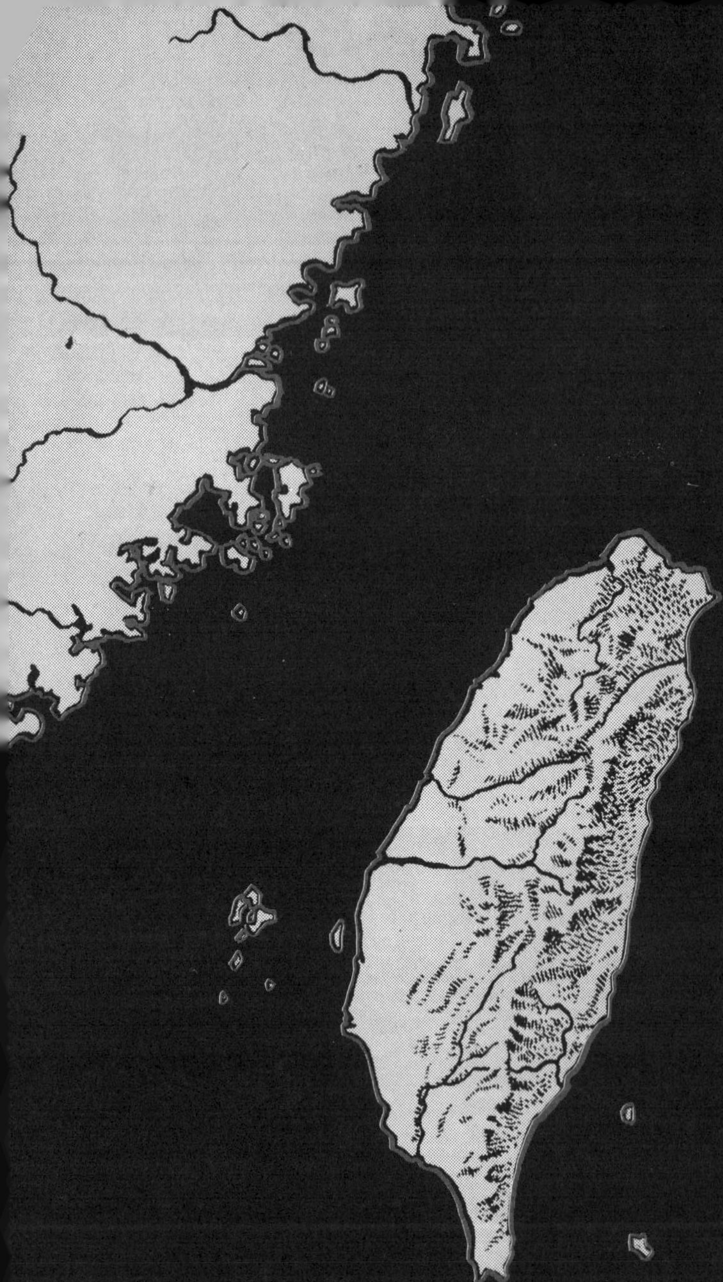

IN FORMOSA'S DIRE

MILTON CANIFF

STRAITS

A COMPLETE STEVE CANYON ADVENTURE

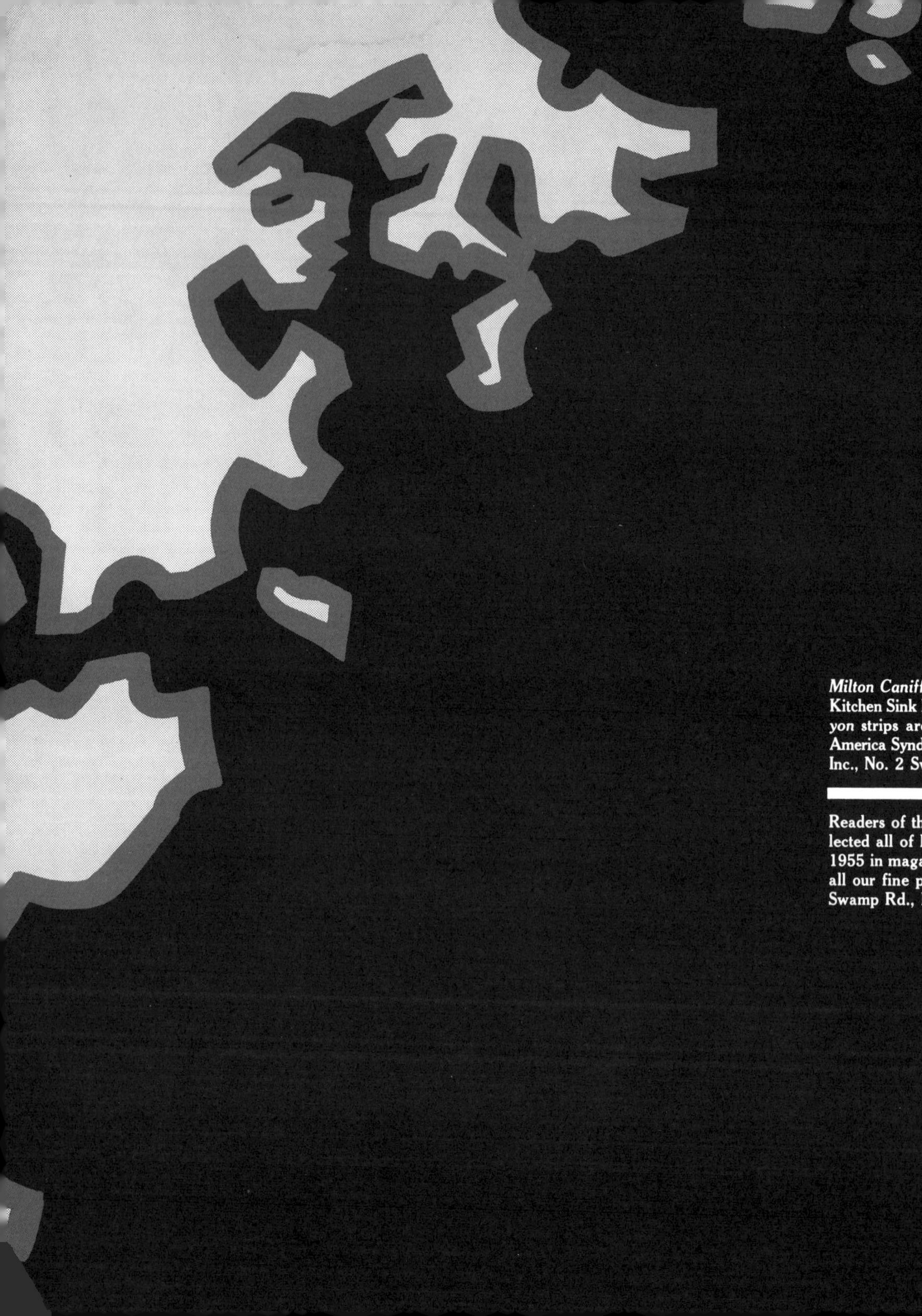

Milton Caniff's Steve Canyon "In Formosa's Dire Straits" is published by Kitchen Sink Press, Inc., No. 2 Swamp Rd., Princeton WI 54968.

ISBN 0-87816-044-2

Denis Kitchen — *Publisher*
Peter Poplaski — *Editor/Art Director*
Dave Schreiner — *Copy Editing*
Ray Fehrenbach — *Production Assistant*
Willie Tuck — *Caniff Studio Manager*
Lucy Caswell — *Ohio State University Milton Caniff Research Center*

Princeton KITCHEN SINK PRESS Wisconsin

STEVE CANYON

CANIFF ON CANIFF

A cartoonist's biography, drawn for *Collier's* magazine in 1948

CHANCE AT HORATIO ALGER-TYPE CAREER SEEMED FOREVER LOST WHEN SUBJECT WAS GRADUATED FROM OHIO STATE UNIVERSITY...
ANOTHER GEORGE BELLOWS?
THE HEAT MUST BE GETTING TO YOU!
1930
HOPE OF 'UP FROM THE RANKS' BACKGROUND REVIVED BY ARRIVAL OF NEW BRIDE AND DEPRESSION ON SCENE AT THE SAME TIME...
WHY ARE YOU SO PALE, DEAR?
5¢
OCCASIONALLY CHERISHED THOUGHTS OF BECOMING AN ACTOR EFFECTIVELY SQUELCHED BY FILL-IN STINT AS MANAGER OF TRAVELING STOCK COMPANY...
ACT 2
BACK TO DRAWING — FOR THE ASSOCIATED PRESS IN NEW YORK — AND THE DISCOVERY THAT THE COMIC STRIP BOYS DON'T KEEP REGULAR OFFICE HOURS...
HENCE THE DREAMING UP OF A FEATURE CALLED 'DICKIE DARE' FOR THE A.P.
STRANGE READING TASTES
QUITE! CHILD PSYCHOLOGY AND UNEXPURGATED ARABIAN NIGHTS
1932
LATER, 'TERRY AND THE PIRATES' FOR THE CHICAGO TRIBUNE — NEW YORK NEWS SYNDICATE, PLUS A SPECIAL STRIP, 'MALE CALL' FOR 3000 SERVICE NEWSPAPERS DURING THE WAR...
HOW DOES THAT Z.I. 4F JOKER LATCH ON TO HOW US GEES YAP?
CANIFF SPY

BUT THE SIMON LEGREE URGE IS DEEP IN EVERY CARTOONIST —HE WANTS TO OWN A CHARACTER OUTRIGHT...
IN THE ADVENTURE STRIP FIELD IT IS ALSO A DESIRE TO IDENTIFY HIMSELF WITH A HANDSOME HERO —SO HE THINKS OF ALL THE THINGS HE WISHES HE HAD DONE
THEN A JEKYLL—HYDE TRANSMUTATION TAKES PLACE! THE IMAGINED IDOL PASSES FROM SKULL TO PAPER
1947
— AND HE FINDS THAT THE SLAVE HE HAS CREATED OWNS HIM!
THINK FAST, BUB! WHAT DO I DO NEXT?
STEVE CANYON
by MILTON CANIFF

FORMOSA, *fawr MOH suh,* or **TAIWAN,** *tie wahn,* a mountainous island, rises from the South China Sea. The stormy Formosa Strait, about 100 miles wide, separates it from China. The wild, forested beauty of the island led Portuguese traders in 1590 to name it ILHA FORMOSA (BEAUTIFUL ISLAND). The Chinese call it TAIWAN (TERRACED BAY). Taipei is the capital and largest city. For location, see CHINA (color map).

Formosa stands on the trade lanes from Indonesia and the Philippines to Japan. Waves of conquerors have swept the island since the early 600's, when the Chinese began to settle its coasts.

When communists overran the mainland of China in 1949, Formosa became the refuge of Nationalist China. Generalissimo Chiang Kai-shek led his defeated forces to the island, and made Taipei the capital of Nationalist China. The United States aided Chiang's government as a barrier to further communist expansion.

The Land and Its Resources

Location, Size, and Description. Formosa, including the offshore islands of Quemoy and Matsu, covers about 13,885 square miles. This is nearly twice the size of New Jersey. Formosa is about 235 miles long and 90 miles wide. It has 1,062 miles of coast. Thickly forested mountains cover two thirds of the land. The ranges, which run north to south, have about 30 peaks rising over 10,000 feet. The highest, snow-tipped Hsin-Kao Shan (Mount Morrison), towers 13,113 feet.

The east coast sheers up from the sea in a line of gray cliffs mounting over 6,000 feet. Short swift rivers slash gorges down to the sea. On the west, the mountains slope to a flat coastal plain about 20 miles wide. Sluggish rivers wind across the lowlands. The Hsilo and Tanshui rivers are the longest streams.

Climate. Formosa's climate is subtropical, with hot

lasts from May to October. A slight earthquake shakes some part of Formosa nearly every day in the year.

The People and Their Work

The People. Formosa has a population of 10,613,000 including about 190,000 *aborigines* (descendants of the earliest known inhabitants). They probably belong to the Malayan and Polynesian group. Two of every three aborigines live in the eastern mountains, hunting and farming. Some of the oldest men wear a chin tattoo, signifying that they have cut off an enemy's head. Head-hunting is now forbidden on the island. Nearly all the rest of Formosa's people are Chinese whose ancestors came from Fukien and Kwangtung provinces. After World War II, about 2,000,000 persons came from the mainland. Most Formosans practice Buddhism or Taoism (see BUDDHISTS; TAOISTS).

In the cities, most people wear Western dress, but many workers go barefoot or wear wooden sandals. Formosan farmers work on hands and knees planting or weeding the rice fields. After harvesting the rice, many farmers spread it on a highway for the traffic to thresh. Others pedal wooden foot threshers. Usually the farmhouse has brick walls and a tile roof. The home faces a courtyard, flanked by thatched outbuildings for poultry and pigs. Nearly all farmhouses have electricity.

Formosa has eight cities with populations over 100,000. They are Taipei (503,086), Kaohsiung or Takao (267,515), Tainan (221,088), Taichung (199,519), Chilung or Kiirun (145,405), Hsinchu (124,596), Chiai (123,819), and Pingtung (108,262). Other cities are Changhua (62,452) and Ilan (37,000). Nearly all the people live on the level coastal plain.

The Formosa entry from the 1963 WORLD BOOK ENCYCLOPEDIA.

Formosa
t 745,000
and. The
The land

average farm has only about three acres. The land requires heavy fertilization.

Formosans work their farms intensively, often inter-

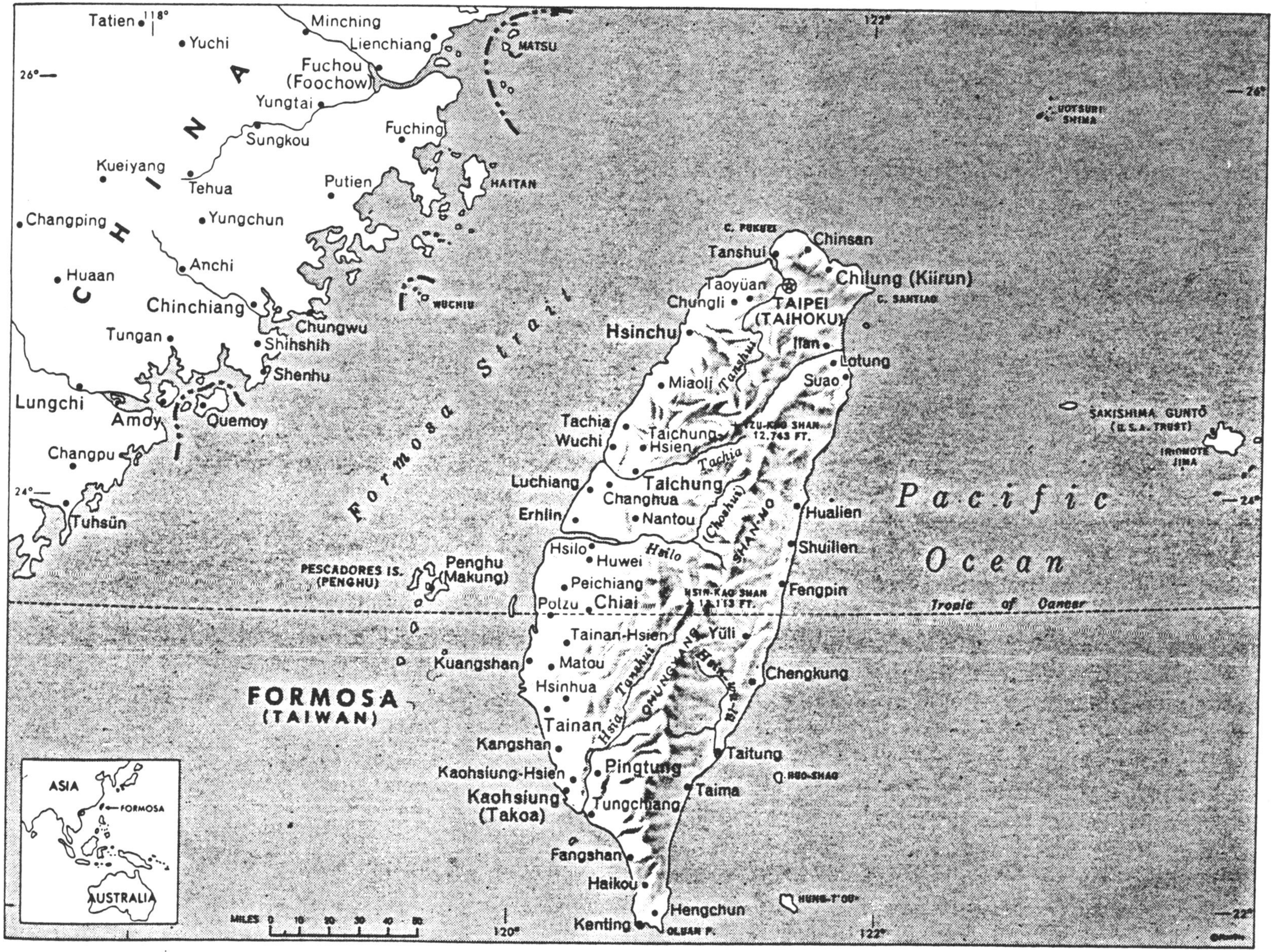

Taipei meets most of the island's need for fertilizer. Other plants produce cement, aluminum, petroleum, flour, paper and other wood products, glass, bricks, and ironwork. Keelung has large shipbuilding yards. Several cities have pineapple canneries, sugar refineries, and tea factories.

provincial assembly, which includes representatives of the aborigines. Assembly members hold office for three years. The duties of the provincial government resemble those of a state government in the United States. The national government administers foreign affairs and the federal departments, such as the department of justice.

STEVE CANYON: February 8th, to August 8th, 1955

2/9
THERE IS A CHANGE IN THE DEPARTURE TIME FOR GREAT CIRCLE AIRLINES FLIGHT 404 WESTBOUND... THE AIRCRAFT WILL BE READY FOR BOARDING AT 1930
AND SO WE GO FROM THE INKY NIGHT TO THE INKY COFFEE POT...
THIS TAKEN, MA'AM?
NO
DON'T LOOK NOW, DOE REDWOOD, BUT THE MAN SITTING NEXT TO YOU USED TO KNOW YOU IN CHINA!
?
MENU
MILTON CANIFF

2/10
STEVE CANYON
WELL, THE LADY REMEMBERS MY NAME... I'M FLATTERED!
I FREQUENTLY RECALL THE NAMES OF TALL, BLOND MEN WITH DARK STREAKS IN THEIR HAIR, WHO SAVE MY LIFE!
THE TIME FLIES BY, BUT YOU GET BETTER LOOKING! COMING OR GOING FROM THE LAND OF REST AND REFRIGERATION?
SWEATING OUT 404 WESTBOUND!
I'M BOARDING —IF AND WHEN! WHAT'S THE TAKE-OFF DELAY?
THE COUNTER MAN CLAMMED UP... WHAT WAS THE 'ACCIDENT' COMING IN?
WHY—AH—STEVE, I THINK THEY'RE CALLING OUR FLIGHT!
MILTON CANIFF

2/11
Copyright 1955, Field Enterprises, Inc.
Registered U. S. Patent Office
OH, MR. CANYON, YOU ARE THE MAN BOOKED FOR THAT SEAT OUT OF HERE!
MY INSTRUCTIONS WERE TO TELL YOU THAT THE PASSENGER IN THE ADJOINING SEAT IS THE ONE YOU WERE EXPECTING
YES, I KNOW. THANKS
DOE! YOU ARE THE INSTRUMENT EXPERT I'M TO RIDE HERD ON!
AND YOU ARE THE AIR FORCE OFFICER WHO IS TO PROTECT ME!
THIS IS DELIGHTFUL—BUT THEY SAID THIS WAS THE SEAT OCCUPIED BY THE PASSENGER WHO HAD AN ACCIDENT ON THE WAY IN! WHAT GIVES?
IT WAS EMPTY BEFORE—THIS MAN SLID INTO IT DURING THE NIGHT...
I BROKE HIS ARM!
MILTON CANIFF

2/12
Copyright 1955, Field Enterprises, Inc.
Registered U. S. Patent Office
I COULDN'T ENLIST TO FLY IN THE KOREAN WAR, STEVE, SO I WENT INTO THE INSTRUMENT PLANT... I HAVE A FLAIR FOR IT, SO BY NOW I AM AN EXPERT...
I KNOW YOU'RE A GOOD PILOT, DOE, BUT DO YOU THINK THE CHINESE AIR CREWS ARE GOING TO LIKE HAVING A WOMAN SHOW THEM HOW TO DO A JOB? IT MAY SEEM LIKE LOSS OF FACE TO BE THE PUPIL OF A WOMAN!
IF OUR MODIFICATIONS OF THEIR PRESENT JETS GIVE THE AIR-CRAFT A BOOST-THEN NO ONE WILL OBJECT TO MY BEING THERE!
I AM TO ESCORT YOU SO THE COMMIES CAN'T KIDNAP YOU AND PICK YOUR BRAINS!
OH-YOU MEN ALL ENJOY THIS CLOAK-AND-DAGGER STUFF! HOW COULD THEY HAVE FOUND OUT WE WERE COMING?
WHO KNOWS?... BUT THE UNOFFICIAL RECEPTION COMMITTEE IS WAITING WITH A RED CARPET—IN THEIR MINDS...
MILTON CANIFF

STEVE CANYON
by MILTON CANIFF
AM I GOING TO HAVE TROUBLE WIT'CHYOU, COL. CANYON? WHAT'S SO ODD ABOUT A WOMAN BEING A TECHNICAL REPRESENTATIVE OF AN AVIATION INSTRUMENT MANUFACTURER?
NOTHING–ESPECIALLY WHEN SHE IS DOE REDWOOD, GIRL PILOT, GIRL EXPLORER, GIRL SMARTIE... BUT—
DOE REDWOOD IS ALSO A GIRL-GIRL –AND I CAN SEE SOME OF THOSE VERY DOWN-TO-EARTH GROUND CREWMEN WHEN YOU SHOW UP ON A MAINTENANCE LINE...
MR. C., YOU FLATTER ME!
A WOLF'S A WOLF, WHETHER IT'S IN ASIA, OR BACK IN MY COMPANY'S PLANT STATESIDE... I THINK I KNOW HOW TO HANDLE THEM BY THIS TIME
YES–I SAW THEM CARRY ONE OFF FLIGHT 404 WHO GOT 'HANDLED' BY REDWOOD!
I GUESS I'M STRONGER THAN I REALIZE... MAYBE THAT'S WHY I'M STILL SINGLE!
TSK! TSK! AND I THOUGHT I WAS SUPPOSED TO BE YOUR BODYGUARD!

OF COURSE THE OBVIOUS LINE IS TO ASK WHO IS GOING TO PROTECT ME FROM YOU?
POSSIBLY THEY THINK YOU SHOULD HAVE A SPARRING PARTNER WHO IS ON THE PAY ROLL—SO YOU WON'T LOSE YOUR SENSE OF TIMING!
I DON'T BUY THE CLOAK AND DAGGER IDEA!... THEY'RE BEING OVER-CAUTIOUS!.. WHAT COULD HAPPEN TO ME IN THE MIDST OF A FRIENDLY CITY?
THAT'S PROBABLY WHAT JULIUS CAESAR SAID TO HIMSELF JUST BEFORE HE GOT IT IN THE 'IDE'
ANYBODY WHO USES PUNS NEEDS PROTECTION FROM ME!
TO THE INN OF THE LUTE, DRIVER!
IT IS AS ANTICIPATED — THE AMERICAN INSTRUMENT COMPANY HAS RESERVED SPACE AT THE INN OF THE LUTE FOR ITS VISITING EXPERT —WHO WAS NOT NAMED!
AND THE ONLY ROUND-EYES WHO TOOK PASSAGE FROM THE AIR-PORT TO THAT HOTEL WERE THE LAUGHING MAN AND WOMAN! HOIA!
SOMETIMES THE YANKEE DEVILS DISPLAY A KIND OF CHILDISH INGENUITY!.. WHO WOULD EXPECT THE INSTRUMENT EXPERT TO ARRIVE AS A CAREFREE TOURIST—COMPLETE WITH WIFE?
HER PRESENCE MAY CAUSE US TROUBLE IN SPIRITING HIM AWAY TO EXTRACT THE SECRETS OF THE NEW DEVICE!
Copyright 1955, Field Enterprises, Inc.
2-13

2/14
Copyright 1955, Field Enterprises, Inc.
FORMOSA
IT IS AS INDICATED! THE YANKEE INSTRUMENT EXPERT ARRIVES AND IS DRIVEN TO THE INN OF THE LUTE! POSING AS A TOURIST AND HIS WIFE DECEIVES US NOT AT ALL!
THE WIFE MAY SERVE TO BLOCK OUR PURPOSE MOMENTARILY, BUT WE SHALL HAVE THE MAN TELLING THE SECRET OF THE NEW INSTRUMENTS BEFORE MANY DAYS!
YOU HAVE RESERVATIONS IN THE NAME OF MY COMPANY!
OH, YES, OF COURSE ... IF YOU WILL PLEASE SIGN THE REGISTER ...
MILTON CANIFF
AND WOULD YOU AND MR. REDWOOD CARE TO GO TO YOUR ROOMS AT ONCE?
BUT I HAVE SEEN IT IN THE YANKEE CINEMA... AMERICA IS RULED BY WOMEN — I THOUGHT THEY HAD PROBABLY TAKEN OVER REGISTERING FOR THEIR HUSBANDS IN HOTELS...

2/15
Copyright 1955, Field Enterprises, Inc.
PERMIT ME, COLONEL CANYON! I AM O. WO OF SECRET POLICE! STUPID CLERK FAILED TO SEE OBVIOUS! COL. CANYON AN' MIZ REDWOOD NO YANKEE MARRIED COUPLE! YOU ARE CARRYING HER COAT!
HEREWITH DOMICILE OF COL. CANYON...
MILTON CANIFF
NEXT DOOR IS DOMAIN OF MIZ REDWOOD...
INSIDE SAME WILL DWELL SECRET POLICEMAN, FEMALE — POSING AS MAID — TO PROTECT GUEST FROM EVIL... ALL TYPES!

Copyright 1955, Field Enterprises, Inc. Registered U.S. Patent Office.
2/16
DOE, IF YOU'VE HAD ENOUGH TIME TO RELAX AND REFRESH, WE'D BETTER MAKE PLANS FOR YOU TO REPORT TO THE JET BASE!
AFFIRMATIVE, BOSS! SHOULD I WEAR MY MOST FETCHING COVERALLS, OR PRETEND TO BE SOFT AND FEMININE?
SINCE I PLAN TO SHANGHAI YOU FOR LUNCH, WEAR THE PRETTIES FOR ME! —AND GIVE THE LOCAL BOYS A TREAT AT THE SAME TIME!
I'LL JUST DO THAT, PARTNER! HOW'S ONE O'CLOCK FOR LUNCH?
MILTON CANIFF
FINE FOR ME!
SUITS ME TOO, PLEASE! THANK YOU VER-RY NICELY!

Copyright 1955, Field Enterprises, Inc. Registered U.S. Patent Office.
2/17
CANYON! —BOOM CANYON!
HELLO, TIMBER-R! MISS REDWOOD, THIS IS TIMBER LYONS, PROFESSOR OF PLUMBING IN THE AIR TRAINING COMMAND!
STEVE MEANS I TEACH JET FLYING TO THE NATIONALIST CHINESE FLIGHT CADETS, MISS REDWOOD
MISS REDWOOD UNDERSTANDS, TIMBER! SHE IS A JET INSTRUMENT EXPERT!
WELL, SEE YOU AROUND — WE HAVE A DATE WITH THE ENGINEERING OFFICER AT THE BASE...
I WOULDN'T MIND SO MUCH THAT CANYON SHOULD TRY TO KEEP US AWAY FROM THE GAL, BUT USING SUCH A WEAK GAG AS HER BEING A JET INSTRUMENT EXPERT!
MILTON CANIFF

2/18
Copyright 1955, Field Enterprises, Inc.
Registered U.S. Patent Office
OF COURSE, COLONEL
IT IS SUCH A PLEASURE TO HAVE YOU WITH US, MISS REDWOOD... NOW IF YOU WILL EXCUSE COL. CANYON AND ME FOR ONE MOMENT-
COL. CANYON, AM I TO BELIEVE THAT YOUR GOVERNMENT WOULD SEND A WOMAN FOR THIS SO SPECIAL TASK?
MISS REDWOOD IS A LICENSED PILOT AND FULLY QUALIFIED!..YOU HAVE SEEN HER PAPERS!
BUT-WELL, A WOMAN'S PLACE IS BEHIND THE ORCHID DOOR IN HER HUSBAND'S HOUSE!
COLONEL, I HAVE A FEELING SOMEONE FORGOT TO EXPLAIN ALL THAT TO CERTAIN INTERESTED PARTIES IN BOTH OUR COUNTRIES!
MILTON CANIFF

2/19
Copyright 1955, Field Enterprises, Inc.
Registered U.S. Patent Office
AT THE U.S. CONSULATE...
WHERE ARE YOU GOING, HOLLY?
DUTY CALLS, DADDY, DEAR! WHEN MOTHER WENT VISITIN' ACROSS THE ISLAND, SHE TOLD ME TO BE SURE TO LOOK IN ON HER CHARITY CASES IN TOWN!
WELL, DON'T GET INVOLVED IN ANY LOCAL SITUATIONS! — I HAVE ENOUGH TROUBLES THESE DAYS...
WHY, OF COURSE NOT, DADDY, DEAR!
MEANWHILE... AT A NEARBY MILITARY AIR FIELD..
THIS IS THE WAY TO LIVE, DOE! I HAVE A GAL WHO WORKS STEADILY AT THE LOCAL PLANT WHILE I TAKE IT EASY — THEN MEET HER WHEN SHE'S THROUGH IN THE MACHINE SHOP!
I HAVE BEEN BUSY, CANYON —ARRANGING FOR YOU TO TEST-FLY THE CHINESE JETS AFTER I HAVE DONE MY OWN WORK!
MILTON CANIFF

STEVE CANYON
by MILTON CANIFF
OBVIOUSLY THERE IS NO JUSTICE... I HAVE BEEN OUT HERE RISKING MY ONLY AVAILABLE NECK TEACHING CHINESE NATIONALIST KIDS TO JOCKEY JETS...
THEN 'NO SWEAT' CANYON APPEARS ON THE SCENE ESCORTING A BEAUTIFUL DISH WHO IS ALLEGED TO BE A TECHNICAL EXPERT FROM AN AIRCRAFT INSTRUMENT COMPANY...
I ASKED HIM IF HE HAD PULL ALONG THE POTOMAC...
AND HE SAID HE HAD A FRIEND IN A HIGH LEVEL KEY JOB IN WASHINGTON—HE WINDS THE CLOCK IN THE TOWER OF AN OFFICE BUILDING ON CONSTI-TUTION AVENUE!
NOW, LOOK, STEVE! THIS 'BODYGUARD' STUFF CAN BE CARRIED TOO FAR...

I'VE GOT WORK TO DO — AND I DON'T LIKE TO BE FOLLOWED AROUND!
I DON'T BLAME YOU, DOE, BUT THE MAN IN THE STRIPED PANTS ORDERED IT THAT WAY...
WELL, I'M A CIVILIAN — AND I DON'T NEED AN AIR FORCE WATCHDOG WHEN I'M DOING MY JOB!
STEVE! STEVE CANYON!
HOLLY HALL! I THOUGHT YOU WERE IN INDIA!
MY HARD-WORKING DADDY IS ASSIGNED HERE — AND I'M TAGGIN' ALONG! AND WHO IS THIS LOVELY LADY?
HOLLY, THIS IS DOE REDWOOD... MISS REDWOOD IS A TECHNICAL REPRESENTATIVE FOR ONE OF THE AIRCRAFT INSTRUMENT COMPANIES...
WELL I DECLARE! HOW VERY EXCITING! WON'T Y'ALL COME AN' HAVE LUNCH AT OUR HOUSE?
SO KIND OF YOU TO ASK US — BUT COL. CANYON HAS TO GO TO THE AIRFIELD WITH ME AS A SORT OF PROTECTOR... I'M SURE YOU UNDERSTAND!
WHY — OF COURSE!
Copyright 1955, Field Enterprises, Inc.
2-20

2/21
Copyright 1955, Field Enterprises, Inc. Registered U.S. Patent Office.
I DO DECLARE! I CAN'T GET OVER IT, MISS REDWOOD—MEETIN' YOU AND COL. CANYON RIGHT SMACK HERE ON THE STREET!
DOE, HOLLY'S FATHER IS A STATE DEPARTMENT FIELD SERVICE OFFICER
OH, I SEE...
HOW IS HE—AND YOUR MOTHER, HOLLY?
DADDY'S BUSY AS A CAT ON A GRIDDLE—BUT HE'S FITTIN'... AND MY BEAUTIFUL MOTHER IS RIGHT HEALTHY... SHE'S OFF VISITIN' FRIENDS ACROSS THE ISLAND
MILTON CANIFF
IF Y'ALL ARE TOO COMMITTED TO COME TO OUR HOUSE FOR LUNCH, I'LL JUST KEEP PECKIN' AT YOU 'TIL YOU HAVE A FREE DAY!
I DON'T RECKON YOU'LL FIND IT TOO ROUGH A PLACE, MISS REDWOOD... YOU CAN GET SKIN CREAMS AND MOST BEAUTY AIDS RIGHT HERE IN TOWN... WELL, 'BYE NOW!

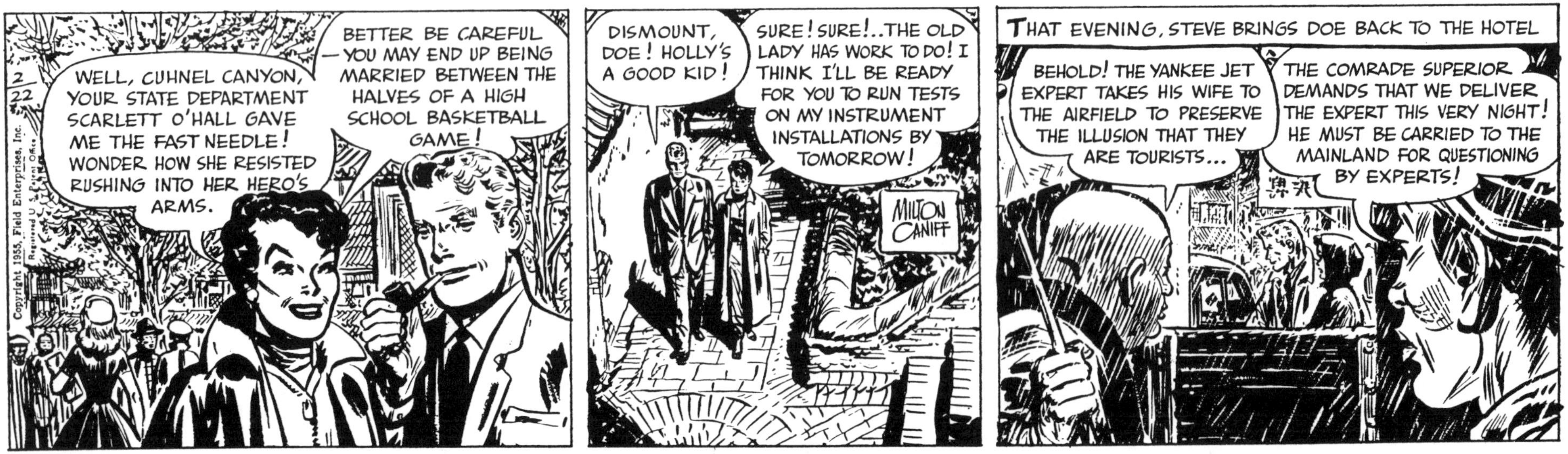
2/22
Copyright 1955, Field Enterprises, Inc. Registered U.S. Patent Office.
WELL, CUHNEL CANYON, YOUR STATE DEPARTMENT SCARLETT O'HALL GAVE ME THE FAST NEEDLE! WONDER HOW SHE RESISTED RUSHING INTO HER HERO'S ARMS.
BETTER BE CAREFUL—YOU MAY END UP BEING MARRIED BETWEEN THE HALVES OF A HIGH SCHOOL BASKETBALL GAME!
DISMOUNT, DOE! HOLLY'S A GOOD KID!
SURE! SURE!.. THE OLD LADY HAS WORK TO DO! I THINK I'LL BE READY FOR YOU TO RUN TESTS ON MY INSTRUMENT INSTALLATIONS BY TOMORROW!
MILTON CANIFF
THAT EVENING, STEVE BRINGS DOE BACK TO THE HOTEL
BEHOLD! THE YANKEE JET EXPERT TAKES HIS WIFE TO THE AIRFIELD TO PRESERVE THE ILLUSION THAT THEY ARE TOURISTS...
THE COMRADE SUPERIOR DEMANDS THAT WE DELIVER THE EXPERT THIS VERY NIGHT! HE MUST BE CARRIED TO THE MAINLAND FOR QUESTIONING BY EXPERTS!

2/23
Copyright 1955, Field Enterprises, Inc.
Registered U. S. Patent Office
CHINA AIR FORCE OFFICER BELOW STAIR-SIDE, COLONEL CANYON! HE SAY MOST IMPORTANCE TO SPEAK WITH YOU ALONE!
COP ON DOE'S DOOR AND A POLICEWOMAN INSIDE WITH HER... SHE'LL BE SAFE ENOUGH...
OKAY! LEAD THE WAY!
THAT'S NOT THE WAY TO THE LOBBY!
QUITE SO! OFFICER DO NOT WISH OBSERVATION! —HE WAIT IN SIDE PARLOR
AH, COLONEL! THANK YOU FOR COMING...
MILTON CANIFF

2/24
Copyright 1955, Field Enterprises, Inc.
Registered U. S. Patent Office
THE EYES OF THE PHONY OFFICER TELEGRAPH THE IMPENDING BLOW
MILTON CANIFF

2/25
Copyright 1955, Field Enterprises, Inc.
Registered U.S. Patent Office
H-HELLO
COL. CANYON? THIS IS HOLLY HALL! I KNOW THINGS MUST HAVE BEEN DULL SINCE YOU'VE BEEN HERE—SO I'M FIXIN' TO HAVE A LUNCHEON ESPECIALLY FOR YOU AN' MISS REDWOOD!
MILTON CANIFF

2/26
Copyright 1955, Field Enterprises, Inc.
Registered U.S. Patent Office
SO NOW, DOE, YOU SEE THE NEED FOR TIGHT SECURITY! THE GOONS WHO JUMPED ME LAST NIGHT MUST HAVE THOUGHT I AM THE INSTRUMENT EXPERT
AND I ACCEPTED THIS DATE WITH HOLLY HALL AND HER DAD SINCE YOU MAY NEED HELP FROM THE U.S. CONSUL— AND YOU SHOULD KNOW HIM!
–MISS REDWOOD! –COL. CANYON! MY! Y'ALL ARE A SIGHT FOR SORE EYES — SURE ENOUGH!
MY DADDY IS SLAVIN' IN THE STRIPED-PANTS DEPARTMENT— SO I'M 'FRAID YOU'RE GONNA HAVE TO PUT UP WITH ONLY LITTLE OL' ME!
MEANWHILE = AT THE U.S. CONSULATE, HOLLY'S FATHER LISTENS
...THERE WAS A MUGGING ATTACK ON AN AIR FORCE SPECIAL PROJECT OFFICER NAMED CANYON LAST NIGHT... ADVISE AMERICAN CIVILIANS TO AVOID CONTACT WITH MILITARY PEOPLE WHOSE JOBS MAKE THEM THE OBJECTS OF VIOLENCE!
MILTON CANIFF

STEVE CANYON
by MILTON CANIFF
I DECLARE—I NEVER HEARD OF ANYTHING SO FASCINATING IN MY ENTIRE LIFE...
JUST THINK OF MISS REDWOOD SHOWING THOSE MECHANICS HOW TO MAKE THE JET AIRPLANES GO FASTER!
I MERELY SHOW THEM HOW TO ADJUST THIS NEW INSTRUMENT MY COMPANY MADE TO STEP UP THE EARLIER MODELS
IMAGINE A PRETTY GIRL DOING ALL THAT! I SWEAR I CAN'T EVEN USE A PENCIL SHARPENER PROPERLY! I AM SO IMPRESSED I CAN JUST BARELY SPEAK!...
STEVE, I DON'T LIKE TO BREAK UP A PLEASANT INTERLUDE, BUT I AM BOOKED TO MEET THE CHIEF ENGINEERING OFFICER!
THANKS SO MUCH FOR HAVING US TO LUNCH, MISS HALL

YES, HOLLY, YOU'RE A GOOD HOSTESS FOR YOUR DAD!
YOU'RE JUST AN OL' FLATTERER, COL. CANYON! IF MY DARLIN' MOTHER WEREN'T VISITING FRIENDS ACROSS THE ISLAND SHE'D SHOW YOU REAL GRACE! NOW Y'ALL HURRY BACK —Y' HEAR?
A CONFEDERATE PENNY FOR YOUR THOUGHTS, DOE!
A BRIGHT CHILD OF A STATE DEPARTMENT FIELD SERVICE MAN CAN BECOME WELL POISED VERY EARLY IN LIFE...
I WONDER WHAT WILL EVENTUALLY HAPPEN TO HER?
MISS HALL WILL DO VERY WELL FOR HER-SELF...

YOU SOUND AS IF YOU SORT OF RESENT HOLLY!
ME? DON'T BE SILLY! —LET'S GET THIS POW-WOW WITH THE ENGINEER OVER EARLY —WE MIGHT HAVE TIME FOR A COUPLE OF GAMES OF GIN RUMMY!
MEANWHILE
HELLO, HOLLY... SORRY I COULDN'T BE WITH YOU AND YOUR GUESTS —THINGS ARE POPPING AT THE CONSULATE THESE DAYS! HOW DID IT GO?
DADDY!
YOU DON'T HAVE TO TELL ME! THE GIRL WAS EITHER UGLY—OR HER FINGERNAILS WERE BATTERED FROM THAT INSTRUMENT WORK SHE DOES!
2-27

2/28
Copyright 1955, Field Enterprises, Inc. Registered U S Patent Office
OH, DADDY, I'M SO SORRY YOU COULDN'T BE WITH US FOR LUNCHEON —MISS DOE REDWOOD AND STEVE CANYON WERE HERE!
MISS REDWOOD IS IN FORMOSA TO HELP SPEED UP THE NATIONALIST JET AIRPLANES! ISN'T THAT AMAZING?
IT'S AMAZING AND DANGEROUS, HOLLY! DID CANYON TELL YOU HE WAS ATTACKED BY WHAT WE ASSUME WERE RED AGENTS?
LAW ME, NO!
MILTON CANIFF
I HATE TO TELL YOU THIS, HOLLY, BUT WE HAVE ORDERS FOR U.S. CITIZENS NOT TO FRATERNIZE WITH PEOPLE IN THESE 'SENSITIVE' JOBS!
SO YOU MUST NOT SEE CANYON AND MISS REDWOOD AGAIN WHILE THEY'RE HERE!

3/1
Copyright 1955, Field Enterprises, Inc. Registered U S Patent Office
HOW DOES IT CHECK, STEVE?
YOU'VE GOT IT KNOCKED, DOE! —I'M COMING DOWN...
I WOULDN'T CARE TO DOGFIGHT THAT BABY AGAINST THE LATEST MIG, BUT IT HOLDS UP...
WE TESTED JUST IN TIME—WE'RE GOING TO GET SOME BLAH WEATHER!
COLONEL CANYON! —PLEASE, COMES CHIT!
MILTON CANIFF

3/2
Copyright 1955, Field Enterprises, Inc. Registered U. S. Patent Office
Col. Canyon: My father has forbidden me to see you again. Holly Hall
FOR PETE'S SAKE, DOE — WHAT DO YOU THINK OF THIS ?
OH, STEVE - IT'S PATHETIC!
THE CHILD MAY ONLY BE DRAMATIZING HERSELF —BUT THEN AGAIN...
I'LL HAVE TO GO SEE MR. HALL AND FIND OUT WHAT THIS IS ALL ABOUT...
YOUR BODYGUARD-MAID AND DOORMAN ARE THERE, SO YOU'LL BE SAFE! I'LL SEE YOU—WHY ARE YOU GRINNING ?
WONDERING IF DIPLOMATS ARE ALLOWED TO CARRY SHOTGUNS!
MILTON CANIFF

3/3
Copyright 1955, Field Enterprises, Inc. Registered U. S. Patent Office
WHAT'S THE RACKET IN THE HALLWAY ?
MISSY REDWOOD! — DOOR GUARD CATCH PROWLER NEAR ROOM OF COL. CANYON NEXT DOOR--
WHY- IT'S HOLLY HALL! GUARD, THIS IS THE DAUGHTER OF A U.S. CONSULAR OFFICER — LET HER COME TO MY ROOM
MILTON CANIFF
WHAT HAPPENED, HONEY ?
MY DADDY SAYS WE U.S. CITIZENS MUSTN'T FRATERNIZE WITH YOU WHO ARE ON 'SENSITIVE' MISSIONS!
ODD THAT WE WEREN'T NOTIFIED OFFICIALLY— AND YOUR NOTE ONLY MENTIONED STEVE!
YOU READ MY NOTE ?

3/4
OH, MISS REDWOOD, DID YOU READ THE CHIT I SENT STEVE CANYON IN STRICTEST PRIVACY?
YES, HOLLY! HE COULDN'T UNDERSTAND IT — YOU SAID IT WAS ONLY HIM YOU WERE FORBIDDEN TO SEE!
Copyright 1955, Field Enterprises, Inc.
Registered U S Patent Office
STEVE JUST LEFT TO CALL UPON YOUR DAD TO ASK WHAT IT IS ALL ABOUT!
GREAT DAY! MY DADDY WILL SKIN ME ALIVE!
MAYBE I'LL DO IT FIRST! IF YOU WISH TO GO AFTER STEVE CANYON — DON'T LET ME STOP YOU!
MILTON CANIFF
YOU SEEM A LITTLE YOUNG FOR SUCH THINGS, BUT MAYBE THAT'S OKAY OUT HERE! WHAT'S WRONG, HONEY? DON'T YOU KNOW WHAT TO DO WHEN YOU WIN?

3/5
BUMBLERS! FOOLS! MATERIALISTIC APES!
YES, COMRADE
Copyright 1955, Field Enterprises, Inc.
Registered U S Patent Office
ONLY BECAUSE THE PRESENT SITUATION DROVE US UNDERGROUND MUST WE DEPEND ON SUCH AS YOU!
MILTON CANIFF
YOU ASSUMED THE YANKEE, CANYON, TO BE THE JET PLANE INSTRUMENT EXPERT! MEANWHILE THE WOMAN HAS SUPERVISED THE SPEEDING UP OF MULTITUDINOUS AIRCRAFT!
EVEN WHEN YOU TRIED TO ABDUCT THE WRONG PERSON YOU FLUBBED! NOW BRING ME THE YANKEE WOMAN!.... IF YOU FAIL, YOU SHALL NOT HAVE THE LUXURY OF DYING — WE SHALL PEEL OFF WIDE STRIPS OF YOUR SKIN FROM HEAD TO TOE... VERY SLOWLY!

STEVE CANYON
by MILTON CANIFF
ARE YOUR MINDS STILL SO FILLED WITH MIDDLE-CLASS BROMIDICS THAT YOU ASSUMED THE JET INSTRUMENT EXPERT WOULD BE A MAN? IT IS THE WOMAN! THE AMERICAN WOMAN!!
HOLLY, I DON'T THINK STEVE CANYON KNOWS YOU AND I ARE TOGETHER —TALKING ABOUT HIM— IN RELATION TO YOU AND ME!
I DON'T RIGHTLY UNDERSTAND, MISS REDWOOD!
MEANWHILE= DOE REDWOOD'S QUARTERS...
OH, FOR PETE'S SAKE, DON'T ANSWER ME AS IF I WERE YOUR SCHOOL TEACHER!
BUT, MA'AM, I WAS TAUGHT THAT IT IS DISRESPECTFUL TO ADDRESS MY ELDERS AS IF WE WERE THE SAME AGE!
WELL, I ASKED FOR THAT ONE!—BUT LET IT PASS... THE POINT IS, I AM NOT COMPETING WITH YOU FOR THE ATTENTIONS OF COL. CANYON!

PURELY BY ACCIDENT HE WAS ASSIGNED TO ME BECAUSE OF MY JOB! HE IS VERY GOOD COMPANY, BUT THAT ENDS IT!...HE'S ALL YOURS, IF YOU CAN CATCH HIM ...
GRACIOUS ME, MA'AM, I MUST HAVE GIVEN YOU A WRONG IMPRESSION!
I KNOW I COULD NEVER COMPETE WITH A LOVELY, MATURE CREATURE SUCH AS YOU! WHEN YOU TWO ARRIVED I TURNED TO YOU AS I WOULD TO A TRUSTED UNCLE AND AUNT! I DECLARE, I'M JUST CRUSHED THAT YOU THOUGHT I'D PRESUME TO DO SUCH A THING!
YOU PULLED MY FANGS IN ADVANCE.... MAYBE YOU'D BETTER GO HOME BEFORE I BUST OUT CRYING! —OH! IT'S RAINING! AND YOU HAVE NO UMBRELLA! HERE—TAKE MY COAT!..IT HAS A HOOD—SO YOU WON'T SPOIL YOUR BONNET!
I SWEAR I DON'T KNOW HOW TO THANK YOU FOR BEIN' SO SWEET!
BELIEVE ME, HONEY, I'M NOT THE SWEET TYPE! NOW HURRY BEFORE YOUR DAD STARTS WORRYING! TAKE A TAXI!
415
BEHOLD! THE WOMAN EXPERT EMERGES ALONE! I REMEMBER THE RED RAIN CLOTHING! THIS IS OUR CHANCE!.. GET HER!
Copyright 1955, Field Enterprises, Inc.
3-6

3/7
Copyright 1955, Field Enterprises, Inc
HELLO, CANYON! — GLAD TO SEE YOU!
I'M HAPPY TO SEE YOU, TOO, MR. HALL, BUT I'M DISTURBED BY A NOTE I HAD FROM HOLLY
SHE SAID YOU HAD 'FORBIDDEN' HER TO SEE ME!
HOLLY IS A ROMANTIC AND PROBABLY OVER-DRAMATIC CHILD... I RELAYED THE CONSULATE ORDER THAT U.S. NATIONALS WERE TO STAY AWAY FROM PEOPLE LIKE YOU AND MISS REDWOOD, WHO ARE ON 'SENSITIVE' JOBS!
THE NOTE MUST HAVE BEEN HOLLY'S INTERPRETATION
WELL— THAT'S A RELIEF!
MILTON CANIFF
BUT STEVE WOULD NOT BE RELIEVED IF HE KNEW WHAT WAS HAPPENING TO HOLLY HALL AT THIS MOMENT....
TAXI!
PERFECT! THE YANKEE WOMAN JET EXPERT IS WALKING INTO OUR HANDS!

3/8
Copyright 1955, Field Enterprises, Inc
TAXI! TAKE ME TO THE UNITED STATES CONSULATE!
YES, MISSY
WHGH
WE CAN PUT HER ON BOARD THE JUNK AT ONCE — SO THEY MAY RUN THE BLOCKADE TO THE MAINLAND IN THE DARK!
THEY WILL HAVE HER WORKING OVER JET ENGINE BLUEPRINTS BY MORNING!
MILTON CANIFF

3/9
Copyright 1955, Field Enterprises, Inc. Registered U.S. Patent Office.
MILTON CANIFF
IT IS THE YANKEE WOMAN JET ENGINE EXPERT! TAKE HER ON BOARD AND GET UNDER WAY AT ONCE!
HOLA! THIS IS A PRIZE!
HASTEN, COMRADE! TRANSPORT HER TO THE MAINLAND BEFORE SOMEONE GROWS SUSPICIOUS!
MY CURIOSITY CANNOT WAIT! I MUST SEE THE FEMALE WHO POSSESSES SUCH KNOWLEDGE!
DO NOT REMOVE THE GAG! SHE WILL CRY OUT AND BE HEARD ON SHORE!
CONSIDER THIS! SHE IS PRETTY —BUT VERY YOUNG!
PSST! THE JET EXPERT HAD RAVEN BLACK HAIR! THE RAIN CLOTHING IS HERS, BUT WE HAVE DELIVERED THE WRONG FEMALE! WALK, DO NOT RUN TO THE NEAREST EXIT!

3/10
Copyright 1955, Field Enterprises, Inc. Registered U.S. Patent Office.
MILTON CANIFF
HASTEN TO THE CHINA MAINLAND, COMRADE! THE ALARM FOR THE YANKEE WOMAN JET EXPERT WILL SOON BE SOUNDING!
IT IS SO! GO ASHORE AND BACK TO YOUR UNDERGROUND DUTIES!
DO NOT APPEAR TO PANIC BECAUSE WE DELIVERED THE WRONG FEMALE!
EYEYA! A BULLET FROM THE JUNK COULD STILL REACH US SO EASILY
WE ARE OUT OF EARSHOT OF THE PORT! REMOVE THE GAG!
IF I WEREN'T SO JELLY—LEG SCARED I'D BE LAUGHIN' OUT LOUD AT WHAT YOU'RE DOIN'!
THIS IS WHAT MAKES IT SO TRYING TO FIGHT THESE PEOPLE — NOT ONLY IS THE YANKEE JET EXPERT A WOMAN-CHILD, BUT SHE GIGGLES WHEN SHE IS SUPPOSED TO SWOON!

3/11
Copyright 1955, Field Enterprises, Inc. Registered U.S. Patent Office
MISTER, I DON'T KNOW A LIVELONG THING ABOUT JET INSTRUMENTS! I AM HOLLY HALL, DAUGHTER OF HOMER HALL OF THE U.S. CONSULATE!
QUICK THINKING TO LEAD US OFF THE TRACK! —BUT YOU WILL TALK, MISS—YOU WILL TALK!
MEANWHILE = HOLLY'S FATHER HAS NOT YET LEARNED SHE IS MISSING—BECAUSE OF THE INTERNATIONAL CRISIS AND HIS WORK IN THE U.S. CONSULATE...
HALL, TAKE CARE OF THIS! A STATESIDE FIRM WANTS ACCURATE FIGURES ON HOW MANY GIRLS ON FORMOSA USE LIPSTICK!
WHILE STEVE CANYON IS HELPING WITH THE SUCCESS OF THE JET INSTRUMENT PROGRAM...
MILTON CANIFF
SEND A DOZEN OF THOSE TO MISS DOE REDWOOD AT THE INN OF THE LUTE...

3/12
Copyright 1955, Field Enterprises, Inc. Registered U.S. Patent Office
HINGLING, COL., CANYON WILL STOP BY IN A LITTLE WHILE...
SO, MISSY REDWOOD
MILTON CANIFF
SOMETHING WRONG, HINGLING?
NOT MY BUSINESS, MA'AM, BUT BOOK ON TURBO COMPOUND DEVICES ODD WAY TO PREPARE FOR VISIT OF HANDSOME MAN!
YOU'RE RIGHT, MOTHER CHINA! WILL YOU BRING ME MY RED SWEATER—THE ONE THAT SHRANK?

STEVE CANYON®
BY MILTON CANIFF
BUT I TELL YOU I DON'T KNOW ABOUT ANY OL' JET INSTRUMENTS! GREAT DAY, MISTER, WHAT MUST I DO TO PROVE TO YOU THAT I AM HOLLISTER HALL! MY DADDY IS A UNITED STATES CONSULAR OFFICIAL!
WHAT WILL OUR COMRADE SUPERIORS DO TO US WHEN THEY LEARN WE SEIZED THE WRONG AMERICAN FEMALE?
THAT SHE WAS WEARING THE REDWOOD ONE'S RAIN CLOTHING WILL NOT SAVE US...
THE COMRADES WILL NOT LEARN OF THE ERROR UNTIL THERE IS PUBLIC ANNOUNCEMENT OF THE REAL IDENTITY OF THE ABDUCTED GIRL...
MEANWHILE THEY WILL HAVE TAKEN THE WOMAN-CHILD TO THE CHINA MAINLAND —AND IF YOU AND I ARE SMART WE SHALL SOON BE ON OUR WAY TO TIMBUCTU!
OUTER TIMBUCTU!

MEANWHILE = HOLLY'S FATHER IS SO BUSY WITH THE EXPLOSIVE DIPLOMATIC SITUATION THAT HE DOES NOT KNOW SHE HAS NOT RETURNED HOME... AND AT DOE REDWOOD'S HOTEL...
KNOCK! KNOCK! I SEE YOU WEREN'T KIDNAPPED WHILE I WAS AWAY... MISS R.
NOT MUCH CHANCE, KEEPER CANYON...
WITH A NATIONALIST SECRET POLICE-WOMAN IN THE NEXT ROOM AND A GUARD IN THE HALL OUTSIDE, I'M WELL PROTECTED!
THE INTELLIGENCE BOYS JUST TOLD ME THEY HEAR THE COMMIES ARE SWEATING BECAUSE YOUR INSTRUMENT INSTALLATIONS ON THE NATIONALIST JETS ARE SHOWING TEST FLIGHT RESULTS! CONGRATULATIONS!
WHILE BACK ON THE BOAT—BOUND FOR THE RED CHINA MAINLAND...
WE HAVE BLUE-PRINTS OF THE U.S. JET ENGINES USED BY THE IMPERIALIST FORCES!
YOU WILL SHOW US HOW YOUR NEW INSTRUMENT STEPS UP THE SPEED OF THIS TYPE POWER PLANT!
HONEST, MISTER! I DECLARE I COULDN'T MAKE A WORKIN' DRAWIN' OF A BOBBY PIN!
...BAMBOO DRIVEN BENEATH YOUR FINGERNAIL MIGHT DECIDE YOU TO TELL US ABOUT THE JET INSTRUMENTS!
Copyright 1955, Field Enterprises, Inc.
3-13

3/14
Copyright 1955, Field Enterprises, Inc. Registered U. S. Patent Office.
THINKING THEY HAVE DOE REDWOOD ABOARD, THE RED JUNK'S CREW STARTS TO BEAR DOWN ON THE TERRIFIED HOLLY
DO NOT PRETEND IGNORANCE, WOMAN! THESE CREWMEN ARE SAILORS, BUT I AM AN ENGINEER! YOU MAY BE AS TECHNICAL AS YOU LIKE!
MILTON CANIFF
MISTER, I COULD BARELY PASS HIGH SCHOOL ALGEBRA! I'M NOT ONLY STUPID BUT SCARED OUT OF WHAT WITS I DID HAVE!
MEANWHILE = STEVE AND DOE REDWOOD KNOW NOTHING OF HOLLY'S PLIGHT...
STEVE, IT WAS SWEET OF YOU TO SEND THE FLOWERS!
THE CHINESE SAY "AN OFFICIAL NEVER FLOGS A BEARER OF GIFTS"!
DO I HAVE A REASON TO FLOG YOU, EVEN IF I HAD THE RIGHT? HOLLY CAME TO SAY YOU WERE JUST AN UNCLE TO HER — PERHAPS THOU BOTH "DOTH PROTEST TOO MUCH"...

3/15
Copyright 1955, Field Enterprises, Inc. Registered U. S. Patent Office.
DOE, YOU DON'T REALLY THINK A KID LIKE HOLLY HALL COULD MEAN ANYTHING TO ME, DO YOU?
IN THE FIRST PLACE, I DON'T CARE—IN THE SECOND, JULIET WAS ONLY FOURTEEN!
I GUESS YOU'RE PULLING MY LEG —AND I'M BITING ON THE GAG! I MUST HAVE A CONSCIENCE! —MAYBE I DO LIKE HOLLY!
THAT CERTAINLY WAS A LIFE STORY IN ONE PARAGRAPH!
MILTON CANIFF
SORRY, DOE — I DIDN'T MEAN TO BORE YOU WITH SMALL TALK!
I WAS JUST THINKING THAT A RAINY EVENING SUCH AS THIS IS NO TIME FOR ANY KIND OF CONVERSATION!

3/16
Copyright 1955, Field Enterprises, Inc.
Registered U.S. Patent Office.
HOLD THE PRESSES WHILE WE REVIEW THE BIDDING...
DOE, I HAVE COME INTO STRANGE AIRPORTS ON RAINY NIGHTS...AND ALMOST PILED UP BY THINKING I SAW APPROACH LIGHTS WHEN IT WAS REALLY SOMETHING ELSE...
MILTON CANIFF
JUST NOW YOU SAID "THIS IS NOT A NIGHT FOR ANY KIND OF CONVERSATION"
WHICH COULD MEAN —"GO, SCHMO!" ...OR—
IT'S A GOOD THING ALL AMERICANS HAVEN'T BEEN AS CAUTIOUS AS YOU —OR CALIFORNIA WOULD STILL BELONG TO SPAIN!

3/17
Copyright 1955, Field Enterprises, Inc.
Registered U.S. Patent Office.
SAY, DOE—JUST WHAT ARE THOSE INSTRUMENTS YOU CAME HERE TO INSTALL?
I DON'T REMEMBER!
MILTON CANIFF

3/18
Copyright 1953, Field Enterprises, Inc.
AH—HMM... MISSY REDWOOD!
TELEPHONE RINGS!
OH—AH—YES... THANK YOU, HINGLING
HELLO...THIS IS SHE SPEAKING! OH, HOW DO YOU DO, MR. HALL! WHY, NO—HOLLY LEFT HERE HOURS AGO...
AND SO THE STORY BREAKS THAT HOLLY HAS DISAPPEARED...
AND IN THE FORMOSA STRAITS
FOR THE 'LEVEN MILLIONTH ...T-TIME, MISTER, I KNOW NOTHIN' ABOUT J-J-JET ENGINES.
MILTON CANIFF

3/19
SHE HAS FAINTED AGAIN, COMRADE!
THE SUSPICION GROWS TO BELIEF—THAT OUR AGENTS ON FORMOSA SENT US THE WRONG FEMALE!
IF WE ADMIT THIS ON THE MAINLAND WE SHALL NOT SEE ANOTHER SUN!
STEER A NEW COURSE—WHILE WE ALL THINK—HARD!
MILTON CANIFF
AND AMONG THE OTHER RESULTS OF THE DISCOVERY OF HOLLY'S DISAPPEARANCE... AT A POLICE STATION...
SIRE, DO YOU THINK THE REDS ABDUCTED THE DIPLOMAT'S DAUGHTER?
WHY SHOULD THEY? THE ONE I WILL QUESTION IS THE YANKEE COLONEL! SEND FOR HIM!

STEVE CANYON
by MILTON CANIFF
IT IS IMPOSSIBLE THAT A SOFT WESTERN FEMALE COULD WITHSTAND SUCH PERSUASION! I AM NOW CONVINCED THAT SHE IS NOT THE U.S. JET INSTRUMENT EXPERT!
OUR AGENTS BUNGLED...
SHE WILL BE IN THE WAY! SHALL WE THROW HER INTO THE SEA?
THAT MIGHT BE BEST!
MEANWHILE = BACK ON FORMOSA...
YOU MUST CALM DOWN, MR. HALL!
I BLAME MYSELF FOR THIS! I NEVER SHOULD HAVE FORBIDDEN HOLLY TO SEE STEVE CANYON!
STEVE, THIS IS MY FAULT — MAYBE HOLLY DID SOMETHING RASH AFTER SHE LEFT ME!
SHE'S TOO WELL ADJUSTED, DOE! I HAVE A DATE WITH THE POLICE! MAYBE THEY'VE HIT ON A LEAD!

COL. CANYON, THIS CHIT IN THE HAND-WRITING OF MISS HALL READS= "COL. CANYON = MY FATHER HAS FORBIDDEN ME TO SEE YOU, (SIGNED) HOLLY HALL"
WAS MISS HALL IN LOVE WITH YOU, COLONEL?
ALL U.S. NATIONALS WERE WARNED TO AVOID US MILITARY PEOPLE IN SENSITIVE JOBS! HOLLY MAY HAVE BUILT THIS INTO A BIG, PERSONAL DENIAL!
YOU DID NOT ANSWER MY QUESTION, COLONEL!
HOLLY IS A ROMANTIC CHILD—SHE MAY HAVE IMAGINED HERSELF IN LOVE WITH ME...STUFFY AS IT SOUNDS FOR ME TO SAY SO!
WHILE ON A U.S. NAVAL VESSEL IN THE STRAITS OF FORMOSA...
WE ARE TO LOOK FOR A VESSEL ON WHICH THE DIPLOMAT'S DAUGHTER MAY BE A PRISONER!
THAT'S JOLLY! WE HAVE NOTHING ELSE TO DO OUT HERE EXCEPT HUNT FOR WANDERING DEBUTANTES!
—AND ON A COMMERCIAL AIRLINER CROSSING FORMOSA...
THE WOMAN WITH SILVER HAIR IS MRS. HALL, MOTHER OF THE GIRL WHO DISAPPEARED!
I KNOW!.. AND I THINK I HAVE TROUBLES? I JUST REALIZED MRS. HALL IS BLIND!
CAT
Copyright 1955, Field Enterprises, Inc. 3-20

3/21
Copyright 1955, Field Enterprises, Inc. Registered U. S. Patent Office.
MY WIFE IS ON THAT PLANE —SHE'S BLIND! --I---
OH, YES, MR. HALL—STEP THROUGH HERE---
GIL! IT'S BETTER NOW THAT YOU'RE HERE! IT'S ALL MY FAULT THAT HOLLY DISAPPEARED! YOU SEE--
HOMER, HONEY, I'M CERTAIN SURE YOU DID WHAT WAS RIGHT—SO DON'T TAKE ON!
I'LL JUST BET THAT WHEREVER OUR HOLLY IS — SHE'S EITHER CALLING THE REEL—OR FIXIN' TO!
AND PERHAPS HOLLY'S MOTHER IS RIGHT! —BECAUSE ON BOARD THE RED JUNK...
ONE MORE TRY TO MAKE HER TELL ABOUT THE JET INSTRUMENTS!
MISTER, I'M NOT BRAVE, I'M ONLY DUMB! I'D TELL YOU TO GET YOU TO STOP! I DON'T RIGHTLY KNOW WHICH END OF THE JET MAKES THE THING GO!
MILTON CANIFF

3/22
Copyright 1955, Field Enterprises, Inc. Registered U. S. Patent Office.
STEVE, ANYTHING NEW ON HOLLY HALL?
NOTHING, DOE, EXCEPT THAT THE POLICE SUSPECT ME OF SOMETHING—IN A VAGUE SORT OF WAY
BECAUSE SHE WROTE YOU THAT FAREWELL NOTE?
RIGHT! HOLLY'S MOTHER IS BACK, WHICH EASES THE STRAIN ON HER DAD...
YOUR FACE LIGHTS UP WHEN YOU MENTION MRS. HALL... SHE MUST BE QUITE A GAL!
GILBERTA HALL IS STONE BLIND—BUT SHE HAS 20/20 INSIGHT! I WISH I COULD SEE AS MUCH OF WHAT'S GOING ON AROUND ME WITH EYES AS SHE SEES WITHOUT THEM!
MILTON CANIFF

3/23
Copyright 1955, Field Enterprises, Inc. Registered U. S. Patent Office.
THE YANKEE FEMALE HAS FAINTED AGAIN —SHALL I THROW WATER IN HER FACE?
I AM EXHAUSTED FROM THE INTERROGATION —WE GO ABOVE AND TAKE FOOD!
COMRADE LO, GUARD HER WELL!
WITH HER BACK TO THE GUARD, HOLLY SLIPS THE SOFT LEATHER DRESS BELT FROM AROUND HER WAIST...
THEN, USING THE METAL TONGUE OF THE BUCKLE, SHE STARTS DOING SOMETHING TO THE LEATHER AT THE OTHER END
MILTON CANIFF

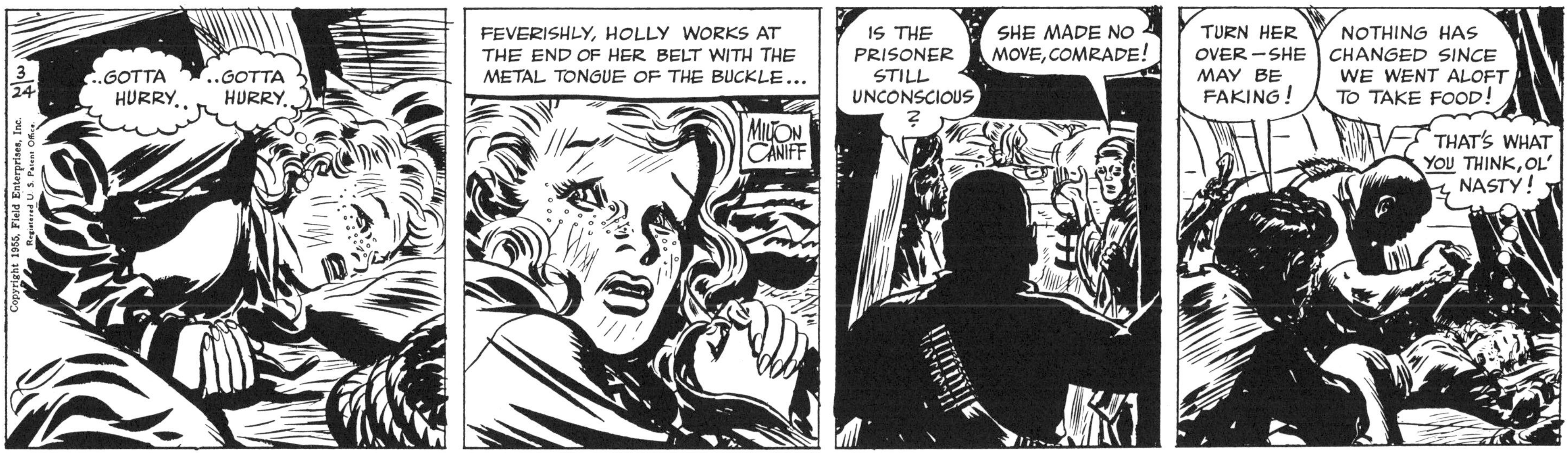
3/24
Copyright 1955, Field Enterprises, Inc. Registered U. S. Patent Office.
..GOTTA HURRY..
..GOTTA HURRY..
FEVERISHLY, HOLLY WORKS AT THE END OF HER BELT WITH THE METAL TONGUE OF THE BUCKLE...
MILTON CANIFF
IS THE PRISONER STILL UNCONSCIOUS?
SHE MADE NO MOVE, COMRADE!
TURN HER OVER—SHE MAY BE FAKING!
NOTHING HAS CHANGED SINCE WE WENT ALOFT TO TAKE FOOD!
THAT'S WHAT YOU THINK, OL' NASTY!

3/25
Copyright 1955, Field Enterprises, Inc. Registered U.S. Patent Office.
I DO DECLARE, GENTLEMEN, I RECKON I KNOW THE ANSWER!
SHE SPEAKS!
THE YANKEE WOMAN JET EXPERT WILL TALK AT LAST!
NO! NO! I RECKON I HAVE THE ANSWER TO HOW YOU CAN SAVE FACE, EVEN THOUGH YOU GOT THE WRONG GIRL
DOE REDWOOD IS THE EXPERT! I WORE HER RAINCOAT, AND YOUR PEOPLE KIDNAPPED ME BY MISTAKE!
MILTON CANIFF
WHY SHOULD YOU THROW LI'L OL' ME INTO THE OCEAN TO COVER UP YOUR ERROR?!
I CAN SHOW YOU HOW TO MAKE 10,000 UNITED STATES DOLLARS IN CASH AND RETIRE TO SOME NICE NEUTRAL COUNTRY!

3/26
Copyright 1955, Field Enterprises, Inc. Registered U.S. Patent Office.
HOMER, HONEY, YOU MUST SLEEP! FRETTING WON'T BRING HOLLY BACK!
I KNOW, GIL, BUT I CAN'T FORGIVE MYSELF FOR SAYING SHE WASN'T TO SEE CANYON... A FINE DIPLOMAT I AM!
COL. CANYON SAYS ALL THE MILITARY AND NAVAL PEOPLE ARE ALERTED ON THE CASE! YOU'LL NEED TO BE RESTED IF THEY WANT YOU IN A HURRY!
IF I CAN FORCE MYSELF TO SLEEP, THEN SURELY YOU CAN! IS THE LIGHT OUT? GOOD NIGHT, DEAR!
YOU'RE RIGHT, OF COURSE —GOOD NIGHT, GIL...
SO HOLLY'S EXHAUSTED FATHER FALLS INTO A HEAVY SLUMBER... AND HER MOTHER'S EYES STARE INTO THE NOTHING OF HER ENDLESS DARKNESS...
MILTON CANIFF

STEVE CANYON
by MILTON CANIFF
MERCY GUIDE ME, GENTLEMEN — IT'S SO SIMPLE...
YOUR PEOPLE ON FORMOSA BROUGHT YOU THE WRONG GIRL!
IT WASN'T YOUR FAULT, BUT YOU CAN'T TURN ME OVER TO YOUR SUPERIORS IN RED CHINA... OR YOU'LL BE SHOT!
BUT YOU'LL ALSO BE SHOT IF YOU DON'T COME BACK WITH THE GIRL JET ENGINE EXPERT...
SO WHY NOT GET RANSOM MONEY FOR ME — AND GO SOME-PLACE ELSE ON THE CASH YOU RECEIVE?
YOU COULD TAKE A PIECE OF MY PERSONAL CLOTHING TO SHOW MY WEALTHY PARENTS — THEY'D PAY UP IN NO TIME!
I'LL WRITE A NOTE SAYING I AM SAFE AND WELL—AND TELLING THEM TO SEND A LOT OF MONEY— IN U.S. DOLLARS...

MY DADDY COULD TAKE THE MONEY ABOARD A SMALL BOAT— BRING IT TO YOU AT SEA — HAUL ME ASHORE, AND YOU COULD BE OFF FOR FUN AN' FROLIC!...
GREAT DAY, GENTLEMEN! ISN'T THAT A SIGHT BETTER THAN A FIRIN' SQUAD...?
THE FEMALE IS CORRECT! —IF WE RETURN TO OUR BASE WE DIE...I WISH TO LIVE!
AYE! YI!
HMMM!
OH, DO SOMETHIN' FAST, MISTER — MY POOR DADDY COULDN'T RAISE $10 RANSOM MONEY, BUT IT'S ALL I COULD THINK OF!
NO TRICKS! YOU WRITE NOTE LIKE WE SAY! NO CODE!
OH, NO, SIR! I'M READY!
MINUTES LATER
THERE! SEE! JUST AS Y'ALL DICTATED!... NOW HERE'S MY DRESS BELT TO PROVE IT IS REALLY ME YOU ARE HOLDING!
NO CODE IN THE LETTER, BUT OH, LAWSY, LET THIS BELT GO AROUND THE RIGHT PLACES!
3-27

3/28
Copyright 1955, Field Enterprises, Inc.
STEVE, DO YOU THINK I CAN DO ANYTHING TO HELP MRS. HALL?
THEY'VE BEEN THROUGH PLENTY! GILBERTA HALL WENT BLIND FROM SMALLPOX WHEN THEY WERE ON A REMOTE POST IN JUNGLE COUNTRY —
BUT IT MUST BE WORSE TO THINK OF THEIR DAUGHTER IN HEAVEN KNOWS WHAT DANGER AT THIS MOMENT
ACTUALLY HOLLY HALL IS DEEP IN AN EXHAUSTED SLEEP ON BOARD THE RED JUNK AT THIS MOMENT...
..WHILE A CREW MEMBER SLIPS ASHORE IN THE DARKNESS AND LEAVES A PACKAGE ON THE STEPS OF THE U.S. CONSULATE...
MILTON CANIFF

3/29
Copyright 1955, Field Enterprises, Inc.
MISTA HALL — COMES PACKAGE ON STEPS IN NIGHT-TIME...
P-PLEASE OPEN IT, NAMU... I-I'M TOO JUMPY...
IT'S A NOTE — A RANSOM NOTE — IN HOLLY'S OWN HANDWRITING — AND A LEATHER BELT... IT'S HERS...
YOU'RE ABSOLUTELY SURE OF THE HANDWRITING — AND THAT THE BELT IS HERS?
MILTON CANIFF
YES! YES! BUT WHY DO YOU SMILE, GIL?
NOW THAT WE KNOW SHE IS ALIVE, I FEEL THAT SOMEHOW OUR LITTLE TOWHEAD HAS COMMAND OF THE SITUATION!

3/30
Copyright 1955, Field Enterprises, Inc. Registered U S Patent Office
I CAME AS SOON AS I GOT YOUR MESSAGE MR. HALL ...
THANK YOU, STEVE...WE CALLED TO ASK YOUR ADVICE...
THE BELT OF THE DRESS HOLLY WORE AND THIS NOTE IN HER HANDWRITING WERE LEFT ON OUR DOOR-STEP DURING THE NIGHT...
'MR. HALL TO TAKE 10,000 U.S. DOLLARS... ON SAMPAN TO A RENDEZVOUS 15 MILES NORTH... KILO POINT... 6 A.M. NEXT... CALM DAY...'
OH H-H
YOU ALL RIGHT, MR. HALL— I MEAN, CON-SIDERING ?
YES... I'M JUST WONDERING HOW HOLLY THINKS I COULD RAISE $ 10,000 !
MILTON CANIFF

3/31
Copyright 1955, Field Enterprises, Inc. Registered U S Patent Office
INSPECTOR, THIS NOTE IN MY DAUGHTER'S HAND-WRITING AND THIS BELT FROM HER DRESS WERE LEFT ON OUR DOORSTEP THIS MORNING...
FROM THIS, WOULD DECIDE ABDUCTORS NOT IN CITY BUT ON OPEN WATER!.. MANY BOATS NEARBY—VERY HARD TO FIND WHICH IS GUILTY ONE!
UNITED STATES MILITARY AND NAVAL INTELLIGENCE PERSONS WILL BE MOST INTERESTED TO KNOW RECENT DEVELOPMENTS IN CASE OF DAUGHTER OF CONSULAR OFFICIAL...
WE LEAVE BELT WITH PARENTS-WHILE COLONEL AND SELF TAKE CHIT FOR FINGERPRINTING AND PHOTOSTATING
WELL, INSPECTOR, ARE YOU SATISFIED I HAD NOTHING TO DO WITH HOLLY'S DISAPPEARANCE ?
RESPECTFULLY SUGGEST THAT UNTIL YOUNG WOMAN RETURNS, ALL PERSONS SUSPECT—ESPECIALLY HANDSOME COLONEL WITH OTHER GIRL FRIEND DOUBLY SO—IN SPADES !
MILTON CANIFF

4-1
Copyright 1955, Field Enterprises, Inc.
WHY SO GLOOMY, MISTER? YOU CAN'T GO BACK TO RED CHINA, BECAUSE YOU KIDNAPPED THE WRONG AMERICAN GIRL...
BUT WHEN MY DADDY BRINGS THE $10,000 RANSOM FOR ME, Y'ALL CAN GO TO MANILA OR SOMEPLACE AN' HAVE A BALL!
YOU WON'T HAVE TO WORRY ABOUT THAT SILLY OL' PARTY DISCIPLINE OR ANYTHING...
YOU MIGHT EVEN BECOME CITIZENS AND BE ABLE TO VOTE! MY DADDY SAYS TRADE IS SURE TO BOOM IN THE PACIFIC... MAYBE YOU COULD START A BUSINESS AN' BE A BIG MILLIONAIRE — WITH A STRING OF CARS AN' PRETTY GALS GIVIN' YOU THE EYE...
WHAT'S YOUR TROUBLE, COMRADE?
T-THAT FEMALE IS T-TRYING TO BRAINWASH ME!
MILTON CANIFF

4-2
Copyright 1955, Field Enterprises, Inc.
YES, GIL...
HOMER, YOU MUSTN'T BE SO DOWNHEARTED!... WHEN THE POLICE DECIDE ON A COURSE OF ACTION, WE'LL TAKE IT... IT'S ONLY FITTING!
GIL, BE PRACTICAL! WHERE COULD I GET $10,000 TO PAY HOLLY'S RANSOM?
I REMEMBER YOUR TELLING US ABOUT SOMETHING THAT HAPPENED DURING THE WAR! I DECLARE! THAT JUST MIGHT BE OUR SALVATION... LISTEN---
MEANWHILE = AT THE POLICE STATION
STEVE, WE WANT TO HELP, BUT HOW CAN WE MIX INTO A PURELY LOCAL POLICE MATTER?
I'LL BE FRANK WITH YOU, ALEX... IF HOLLY'S MOTHER AND DAD KNOW THAT WE ARE ALERTED TO FIND HOLLY, THEY MAY GET A HALF-HOUR'S SLEEP SOME NIGHT SOON!
MILTON CANIFF

STEVE CANYON
by MILTON CANIFF
THE RANSOM CHIT FOR THE HALL GIRL CALLS FOR," A SMALL SAMPAN TO WAIT 15 MILES DUE NORTH OF KILO POINT AT 6 A.M. ON THE NEXT CALM, CLEAR DAY! SHOW DOUBLE LANTERNS FORE AND AFT. NO MAST FOR RADIO"
MR. HALL IS TO BE ON BOARD WITH ONLY AN OARSMAN AND 10,000 U.S. DOLLARS IN CASH. A VESSEL WILL COME ALONGSIDE AND AFFECT THE EXCHANGE...
THE EXCHANGE PLACE IS BEYOND POLICE JURISDICTION. HOW COULD EVEN OUR NAVY HELP IF THE SAMPAN MUST STAND ALONE IN OPEN INTERNATIONAL WATERS, UNABLE TO TRANSMIT AN ALERT?
LATER
AND THAT'S THE SCORE, SO FAR, MR. AND MRS. HALL...
WE DON'T EVEN KNOW THE TYPE OF VESSEL ON WHICH HOLLY IS BEING HELD...

HOMER, ARE YOU CERTAIN THAT IS HOLLY'S BELT ?...
I-I THINK SO, GIL... IT'S THAT DARK BLUE, SOFT CHAMOIS-SKIN KIND OF MATERIAL
MAY I HAVE IT ?
STEVE, WOULD THE U.S. NAVY BE FREE TO ENTER INTO THIS SEARCH IF THEY KNEW HOLLY WAS BEING HELD BY REDS ?
OF COURSE! THAT'S WHAT THE FORMOSA PATROL IS THERE FOR!
WHAT MUST APPEAR TO BE A SORT OF RAISED PATTERN ON HOLLY'S BELT IS A MESSAGE SHE HAS PUNCHED OUT WITH SOME BLUNT INSTRUMENT IN BRAILLE!
IT SAYS THAT SHE IS BEING HELD ON A JUNK NAMED THE TEI-TEI. ALL THE CREWMEN ARE UNDERGROUND COURIERS OPERATING FROM FORMOSA TO RED CHINA!
YOU REALIZE, DON'T YOU, WOMAN, THAT IF THIS PLAN FAILS WE SHALL NOT HAVE YOU WITH US FOR LONG!
GULP
YULP!
Copyright 1955, Field Enterprises, Inc.
4-3

4/4
Copyright 1955, Field Enterprises, Inc. Registered U.S. Patent Office.
GIL, ARE YOU CERTAIN THIS IS BRAILLE ON HOLLY'S BELT?... HER KIDNAPPERS SENT IT TO IDENTIFY HER! — WHY?
THEY DIDN'T KNOW IT WAS BRAILLE ANY MORE THAN YOU OR STEVE DID!
BUT HOLLY LEARNED IT TO HELP ME TEACH AT THE BLIND SCHOOL... SHE PROBABLY SOLD THE COMMUNISTS ON SENDING IT WITH THE NOTE...
OF COURSE! SHE KNEW YOU WOULD WANT TO TOUCH YOUR DAUGHTER'S BELT..
MILTON CANIFF
MEANWHILE = ON THE KIDNAP JUNK
WHY, Y'ALL COULD SAIL YOUR JUNK TO AMERICA, ASK POLITICAL ASYLUM, AND MAKE A PILE OF MONEY SHOWIN' OFF THE BOAT AT PORT CITIES...
IF THE RANSOM DOESN'T COME SOON, THAT FEMALE CHILD WILL HAVE THE CREW ASKING HER TO TAKE OVER AS CAPTAIN!

4/5
Copyright 1955, Field Enterprises, Inc. Registered U.S. Patent Office.
HOLLY HALL'S MESSAGE, PUNCHED OUT IN BRAILLE ON HER BELT SO HER BLIND MOTHER COULD READ IT, GIVES US OUR FIRST REAL BREAK...
IT SAYS SHE IS ON BOARD A JUNK NAMED THE TEI-TEI AND THAT ALL THE CREWMEN ARE UNDERGROUND COURIERS FROM FORMOSA TO RED CHINA...
TECHNICALLY IT IS STILL A FORMOSA POLICE MATTER, BUT HERE'S WHERE I HOPE UNITED STATES FACILITIES CAN COME INTO PLAY...
HANK, WILL YOU PUT THIS DISPATCH ON A RADIO FREQUENCY YOU KNOW THE REDS GUARD — IN A CODE YOU KNOW THEY CAN BREAK?
MILTON CANIFF
... AND MORRIE, YOU COUNTER-INTELLIGENCE PEOPLE MUST KNOW WHAT HAPPENED TO THE STUFF THAT WAS TAKEN FROM THE JAPANESE ARMY ON FORMOSA AT THE END OF THE WAR!.. NOW LISTEN...

4/6
Copyright 1955, Field Enterprises, Inc. Registered U. S. Patent Office.
STEVE, THE LONG-RANGE FORECAST MAGICIANS AT AIR WEATHER SERVICE SAY THERE'LL BE LILY-POND WEATHER OFF KILO POINT AT DAWN TOMORROW!
THAT'S FOR US, DOE! ALERT ALL THE PEOPLE INVOLVED! I'LL GET MR. HALL!
WISH I WERE IN ON THE RESCUE, STEVE! I FEEL GUILTY ABOUT HOLLY...
YOU SIT ON THE RADIO AT THE BASE... THINGS MAY GET NOISY
STEVE... WANT TO KISS THE GIRL GOODBYE — LIKE IN THE MOVIES?
YOU'RE SHAKING, DOE!
I COULD SAY IT'S NERVES—OR THAT I'M GETTING A CHILL—OR I COULD STOP LYING AND ADMIT IT'S THE COMPANY...
MILTON CANIFF

4/7
Copyright 1955, Field Enterprises, Inc. Registered U. S. Patent Office.
MR. HALL, THE FORECAST IS FOR A QUIET SEA THIS MORNING! —OF COURSE THE KIDNAP JUNK MAY FAIL TO APPEAR AS AGREED...
THEY KNOW THE NAME OF THE JUNK FROM HOLLY'S BRAILLE MESSAGE, BUT THE POLICE HESITATE TO RUN IT DOWN BECAUSE THEY MIGHT ENDANGER HER LIFE...
GIL, YOU KNOW WHAT TO DO IN CASE — WELL, IN CASE I DON'T COME BACK...
WHY, HOMER HALL, I DO DECLARE, A PERSON WOULD THINK I HAD NO CONFIDENCE IN MY HUSBAND! ...STEVE AND YOU AND HOLLY WILL BE RIGHT HERE TELLING ME ALL ABOUT EVERYTHING IN A MATTER OF HOURS
BRAVE WORDS TO BOLSTER CONFIDENCE, BUT WHEN THE MEN HAVE GONE, MRS. HALL LETS GO... AND TEARS BURN JUST AS HOT IN SIGHTLESS EYES...
MILTON CANIFF

4/8
Copyright 1955, Field Enterprises, Inc. Registered U.S. Patent Office
ALL SQUARED AWAY, STEVE!..THE POWER BOAT WILL TOW YOU TO THE RENDEZVOUS POINT—THEN SHOVE OFF...
THIS COSTUME SHOULD MAKE ME LOOK ENOUGH LIKE A NATIVE OARSMAN IN THE MORNING LIGHT
GOT EVERYTHING, MR. HALL?
YES, STEVE... IF I COULD ONLY GET MY MIND OFF THE POSSIBILITY THAT HOLLY HAS B-BEEN-- W-WELL...
MILTON CANIFF
WHO BESIDES HOLLY COULD SELL RED COURIERS INTO ASKING FOR RANSOM MONEY?..
IF IT HAD BEEN HER MOTHER, GILBERTA WOULD HAVE HAD RED CHINA THREATENING TO BREAK WITH SOVIET RUSSIA!

4/9
Copyright 1955, Field Enterprises, Inc. Registered U.S. Patent Office
DROP YOUR ANCHOR, STEVE! THIS IS THE SPOT WHERE THE RED JUNK IS SUPPOSED TO MAKE CONTACT!
OKAY, ED... WE'RE CASTING OFF!
WHILE THE BLACKED-OUT JUNK LIES A SHORT DISTANCE AWAY, UNSEEN IN THE DARKNESS...
THE RANSOM CRAFT IS AT HAND...
...AND NOT A MOMENT TOO SOON...
WHY, GREAT DAY, GENTLEMEN —HALF THE PEOPLE I KNOW GO OUT FOR CHOW MEIN AND CHOP SUEY! A BRIGHT BUNCH LIKE Y'ALL COULD START A LITTLE BUSINESS ON THIS JUNK AN' HAVE A WHOLE CHAIN OF SALT-WATER RESTAURANTS IN NO TIME AT ALL! YOU'D MAKE MILLIONS!!
MILTON CANIFF

STEVE CANYON
by MILTON CANIFF
SHREWDLY PLANNED, MY FRIEND = A MOTOR LAUNCH TOWS A LIGHT SAMPAN WITH DOUBLE LANTERNS FORE AND AFT INTO POSITION – THEN DEPARTS INTO THE NIGHT... WHILE WE STAND BY FULLY BLACKED OUT!
THE SEA IS LIKE A POND AS THE DAWN REVEALS THE RAFT-LIKE CRAFT CARRYING ONLY AN OARSMAN AND MR. HALL
THERE IS NO RADIO MAST TO TRANSMIT A WARNING
AND NO SURFACE CRAFT WATCHING US... TAKE HER IN!
HOMER HALL?
YES

PASS THE MONEY UP IN THIS BASKET!
LET ME SEE HOLLY FIRST!
SATISFIED?
YES! HERE IS THE MONEY
IT IS ALL HERE! LET THE GIRL DOWN INTO THE SAMPAN!
AT THIS POINT A GREAT BLACK OBJECT RISES FROM THE WATER ON THE FAR SIDE OF THE RED JUNK
SUBMARINE!
BUT BEFORE THE SUBMARINE CAN OPEN ITS HATCHES THE SKIPPER OF THE JUNK CASTS A HOOK INTO THE BOW OF THE SAMPAN, ORDERS HIS ENGINES FULL SPEED AHEAD AND LUNGES AWAY, TOWING THE SMALL CRAFT SO CLOSE ABOARD THAT THE SUB CANNOT FIRE FOR FEAR OF HITTING THE PEOPLE ON THE LIGHT BOAT... A MACHINE GUNNER IN THE JUNK'S STERN KEEPS THE SAMPAN CREW FROM CUTTING THE LINE...
HEAD FOR OPEN SEA!
Copyright 1955, Field Enterprises, Inc.
4-10

4/11
Copyright 1955, Field Enterprises, Inc. Registered U. S. Patent Office.
THE RANSOM NEGOTIATION IS GOING SMOOTHLY... HOLLY IS PUT INTO THE SAMPAN IN EXCHANGE FOR THE BUNDLE OF MONEY— WHEN A LOOK-OUT CRIES—
SUBMARINE!
DADDY! STEVE! WHAT'S HAPPENING?
THE JUNK IS COMING ABOUT TO PUT ITS STERN TOWARD THE SUB—AND THE GRAPPLING HOOK IS TO KEEP US BETWEEN THEM SO THE SUB WON'T FIRE!
I'LL CUT THE LINE!
MILTON CANIFF
HOMER HALL LUNGES TOWARD THE BOW, BUT A HAIL OF MACHINE-GUN SLUGS FROM THE JUNK DRIVES HIM BACK
MEANWHILE— IN THE RADIO ROOM OF THE NATIONALIST CHINESE AIRFIELD WHERE DOE REDWOOD WAITS FOR SOME WORD OF THE RESCUE...
LISTEN! LISTEN!
THE RESCUE SAMPAN IS BEING TOWED TO SEA ON A LINE FROM THE RENEGADE JUNK
ODD THING! VOICE COMES ON INTERNATIONAL DISTRESS CHANNEL

4/12
Copyright 1955, Field Enterprises, Inc. Registered U. S. Patent Office.
REPEAT... RESCUE SAMPAN IS BEING TOWED TO SEA ON A LINE FROM THE RETREATING JUNK
TO VOICE SPEAKING ENGLISH ON DISTRESS FREQUENCY: THIS IS TAIWAN RADIO... IDENTIFY YOURSELF. OVER...
WHOEVER IT IS, SOMETHING HAS GONE WRONG WITH THE RANSOM DEAL...
INFORM THE AMERICAN FLEET OF THIS LATEST TURN OF EVENTS!
BY THE TIME THE NAVY GETS TOLD, IT MAY BE TOO LATE TO DO ANYTHING...
MILTON CANIFF
DOE RUNS TO THE OFFICE OF THE COLONEL IN COMMAND AT THE AIR BASE...
MISS REDWOOD, I---
COLONEL, HAVE YOU LIKED MY WORK WELL ENOUGH TO DO ME A BIG FAVOR? -THANK YOU, COLONEL—NOW---

4/13
Copyright 1955, Field Enterprises, Inc. Registered U. S. Patent Office.
COLONEL, YOU KNOW I AM A QUALIFIED F-51 PILOT! I WANT TO USE ONE OF YOUR AIRPLANES!
BUT WHY, MISS REDWOOD?
I WAS AFRAID YOU'D ASK THAT! THE KIDNAP JUNK IS RUNNING OUT TO SEA, TOWING OUR FRIENDS IN THE SAMPAN!
I'M GOING TO CUT THE TOWLINE BY DRAGGING AN ENGINE HEAD ACROSS IT AT THE END OF A WIRE CABLE!
MILTON CANIFF
I'LL PROBABLY BE SHOT FOR DOING SO, BUT I WILL PHONE THE FLIGHT LINE AND GIVE YOU PERMISSION
OH, THANKS, COLONEL — NOW I WON'T HAVE TO STEAL THE AIRCRAFT AFTER ALL!

4/14
Copyright 1955, Field Enterprises, Inc. Registered U. S. Patent Office.
DOE REDWOOD TAKES OFF FROM A FORMOSA AIRFIELD TRAILING AN ENGINE HEAD WITH WHICH SHE HOPES TO CUT THE TOWLINE WHICH HAS STEVE, HOLLY AND MR. HALL TRAPPED BEHIND THE RETREATING RED JUNK...
WHILE IN THE SAMPAN...
I CAN'T STAND IT, STEVE! ...THAT MACHINE GUNNER IN THE STERN PREVENTS US FROM CUTTING THE TOWLINE...BUT..
OUR SUBMARINE COULD SHOOT DOWN THE JUNK'S SAILS WITH ITS DECK GUN!
THE PIGBOAT MAY BE HOLDING OFF BECAUSE IF IT OPENED FIRE THE JUNK CREW COULD MASSACRE US, OR —
— IT MAY BE PLAYING COZY BECAUSE IT'S A RUSSIAN SUB!
MILTON CANIFF

4/15
Copyright 1955, Field Enterprises, Inc. Registered U.S. Patent Office.
STEVE, WHATEVER DO YOU MEAN THAT IS A RUSSIAN SUB OFF THERE? I THOUGHT---
WHEN WE SET UP THE RANSOM EXCHANGE, THE NAVY WANTED TO AVOID A POSSIBILITY OF AN INTERNATIONAL 'INCIDENT' WITH THE CHINESE REDS OFF THE FORMOSA COAST...
..SO WE REASONED THAT THE RUSSIANS WOULD BE LOOKING FOR THE RENEGADE CHINESE RED COURIER JUNK EVEN HARDER THAN WE WERE—SO WE REPEATED THE RANSOM DEMAND IN A THINLY CODED RADIO MESSAGE ON A CHANNEL WE KNOW THEY GUARD
—YOU MEAN OUR NAVY ALLOWED US TO BE DECOYS FOR REDS CATCHING OTHER REDS? —DON'T THEY CARE WHAT HAPPENS?
I THINK THAT TINY BLACK PERISCOPE YOU SEE ON THE OTHER SIDE OF THE JUNK WILL SURFACE INTO SEVERAL TONS OF U.S. CONCERN WHEN THE RIGHT MOMENT OCCURS!
AS FAR AS I'M CONCERNED, THAT MOMENT IS NOW!
MILTON CANIFF

4/16
Copyright 1955, Field Enterprises, Inc. Registered U.S. Patent Office.
COMRADE, THE RADAR REVEALS THAT YOU WERE RIGHT! A FIGHTER AIRCRAFT APPROACHES FROM THE FORMOSA COAST!
STAND BY TO DIVE IF IT PROVES HOSTILE TO US INSTEAD OF FRIENDLY TO THE OCCUPANTS OF THE SAMPAN!
BUT DOE IN THE F-51 DOESN'T KNOW IT IS A RUSSIAN SUB ON THE SURFACE —SHE CONCENTRATES ON HOW TO CUT THE SAMPAN LOOSE FROM THE RACING JUNK—
MILTON CANIFF
—AS THE LOOKOUT ON THE JUNK SEES HER COMING AND ALERTS EVERY GUN ON BOARD FOR THE IMPENDING ATTACK...

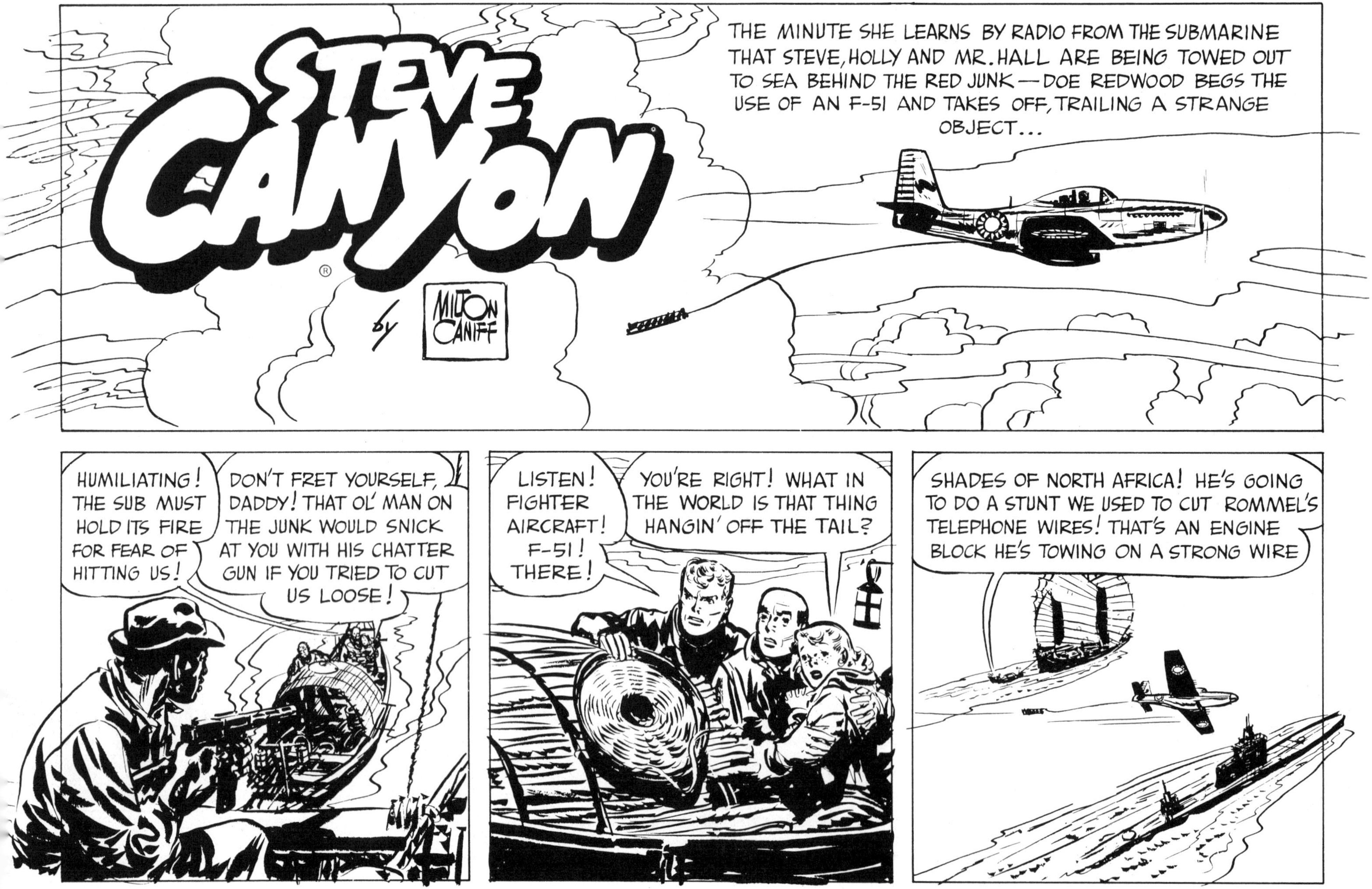
STEVE CANYON
by MILTON CANIFF
THE MINUTE SHE LEARNS BY RADIO FROM THE SUBMARINE THAT STEVE, HOLLY AND MR. HALL ARE BEING TOWED OUT TO SEA BEHIND THE RED JUNK — DOE REDWOOD BEGS THE USE OF AN F-51 AND TAKES OFF, TRAILING A STRANGE OBJECT...
HUMILIATING! THE SUB MUST HOLD ITS FIRE FOR FEAR OF HITTING US!
DON'T FRET YOURSELF, DADDY! THAT OL' MAN ON THE JUNK WOULD SNICK AT YOU WITH HIS CHATTER GUN IF YOU TRIED TO CUT US LOOSE!
LISTEN! FIGHTER AIRCRAFT! F-51! THERE!
YOU'RE RIGHT! WHAT IN THE WORLD IS THAT THING HANGIN' OFF THE TAIL?
SHADES OF NORTH AFRICA! HE'S GOING TO DO A STUNT WE USED TO CUT ROMMEL'S TELEPHONE WIRES! THAT'S AN ENGINE BLOCK HE'S TOWING ON A STRONG WIRE

STEVE DOESN'T KNOW THE PILOT IS DOE! SHE CIRCLES THE THREE VESSELS, THEN LEVELS OFF FOR THE RUN ON THE TARGET...
GUNS BLAZING TO FLATTEN THE PEOPLE ON THE JUNK, SHE BORES IN UNTIL THE TRAILING BLOCK HITS THE TOWLINE AND SNAPS IT CLEAN...
AT ONCE OPEN WATER SHOWS BETWEEN THE NATIVE CRAFT... THE JUNK JAMS ON ALL ITS POWER AND HEADS SEAWARD, WITH THE SUBMARINE RIGHT IN ITS WAKE
BUT THE AIRCRAFT FALTERS—AND DRAGS A WING TIP... THE F-51 CARTWHEELS
AND PLUNGES INTO THE CALM WATER...
RIG THE MAST AND SAIL —I'LL PUMP THIS THING— THAT PILOT WILL BE OUT COLD! HE'LL DROWN!
4-17

4/18
Copyright 1955, Field Enterprises, Inc. Registered U. S. Patent Office.
DOE REDWOOD CUTS THE LINE WITH WHICH THE RED JUNK WAS TOWING STEVE, HOLLY AND HER FATHER OUT TO SEA, BUT HER AIR-PLANE DRAGS A WING AND CRASHES INTO THE SEA...
THE RUSSIAN SUB IS FOLLOWING THE RED JUNK OUT TO SEA...
STEADY THE SAIL SO WE CAN CATCH ALL THE WIND THAT'S BLOWING!
HURRY, STEVE! HURRY, DADDY! THAT PILOT SAVED OUR LIVES!
MILTON CANIFF
THEY DO NOT KNOW THAT THE DOWNED PILOT IS DOE REDWOOD! SOMETHING HAS JAMMED IN THE COCKPIT— SHE CANNOT GET FREE...

4/19
Copyright 1955, Field Enterprises, Inc. Registered U. S. Patent Office.
STILL NO PILOT HITTING THE RAFT! HE'S EITHER HURT OR TRAPPED INSIDE! AT LEAST THE CANOPY WAS JETTISONED!
THE PLANE IS SETTLING INTO THE WATER! HOLLY! GRAB THAT BUCKET!
THERE'S A LENGTH OF HOSE ON THE DECK! CAN YOU ATTACH IT TO THE HAND PUMP AND FORCE AIR THROUGH IT?
GREAT DAY, YES, STEVE! I SEE WHAT YOU'RE GOIN' TO DO!
WE'LL HANDLE IT, STEVE!
STEVE GOES INTO THE WATER, PRESSES THE BUCKET OVER DOE'S HEAD TO FORM A BUBBLE — AS HOLLY AND HER DAD PUMP FRESH AIR TO HER THROUGH THE HOSE...
THE PILOT IS DOE REDWOOD
MILTON CANIFF

4/20
Copyright 1955, Field Enterprises, Inc.
Registered U.S. Patent Office
KEEP PUMPING! SHE WAS TOO KNOCKED OUT TO UNFASTEN HER SEAT BELT!
AS THE AIRCRAFT SINKS, STEVE PULLS THE UNCONSCIOUS DOE REDWOOD FROM THE COCKPIT...
MILTON CANIFF
HE'S GOT HER, DADDY! GREAT DAY IN THE MORNIN'!
...IF SHE'S BADLY HURT WE CAN DO SO LITTLE FOR HER...
BUT MR. HALL HAS FORGOTTEN THE BLACK SPECK ON THE WATER THAT 'WATCHED' THE ENTIRE RESCUE...THE BIG AMERICAN SUBMARINE IT IS THE EYES AND EARS OF, HAS FOLLOWED THE RUSSIAN SUB AND CHINESE RED JUNK, BUT NOT BEFORE IT ALERTED A NAVY RESCUE STATION ON FORMOSA BY RADIO...
NAVY

4/21
Copyright 1955, Field Enterprises, Inc.
Registered U.S. Patent Office
PEACH TREE, THIS IS GINGER 063...I HAVE THE WRECKED AIRCRAFT AND SAMPAN IN SIGHT...THE SEA IS CALM...I AM GOING IN FOR A TOUCHDOWN, OVER
STAND BY TO TOUCH DOWN! GIVE ME A LANDING POSITION CHECK OFF...
NAVY NAVY
MILTON CANIFF
MRS. HALL, THIS IS LT. OVERHAND AT THE NAVY AIR BASE! WE HAVE AN AIR-PLANE PICKING UP YOUR HUSBAND AND DAUGHTER...
AN AMERICAN GIRL PILOT NAMED REDWOOD CRASHED TRYING TO SAVE THEM.... ARE YOU THERE, MRS. HALL?
SORRY, LIEU-TENANT—I JUST COULDN'T SPEAK FOR A MOMENT...
WHILE AT THIS MOMENT A GUARD IS BEING CHANGED AT THE NAVAL HOSPITAL
WHAT'S YOUR NAME, GYRENE?
KIMBERLY

4/22
NAVY AMPHIB CIRCLING TO LAND! YOU'LL BE IN THE HOSPITAL IN NO TIME, DOE!
YOU POOR LAMB —JUST IMAGINE YOU DOIN' THAT FLYIN' FOR ME!
MILTON CANIFF
MEANWHILE = BACK AT THE NAVY HOSPITAL...
MAY I SEE YOUR PASS?
NO PASS
OH, DEAR! MY HUSBAND AND DAUGHTER WILL BE LANDING SOON IN A NAVY RESCUE PLANE! MAY I WAIT AT THE DOCKSIDE, OFFICER?
I'LL ASK, MA'AM!
SHE'S EITHER DRUNK OR TRYING TO FLATTER ME... SHE CALLED ME 'OFFICER'!

4/23
MA'AM, THIS DOCK IS OUT OF BOUNDS TO CIVILIANS
A LT. OVERHAND PHONED TO SAY MY HUSBAND AND DAUGHTER WOULD BE BROUGHT HERE BY A NAVY RESCUE PLANE...
OH, OF COURSE! THAT'S THE MISSION WHERE THE GIRL PILOT CRASHED WHILE HELPING RELEASE THEM! ...MAY I SEE YOUR IDENTIFICATION, MA'AM?
WOULD YOU PICK IT OUT OF MY BAG? I AM BLIND...
I'LL PHONE FOR PERMISSION FOR YOU TO STAY, MRS. HALL
THANK YOU! — AND COULD YOU ASK HOW BADLY HURT THE GIRL WAS? — ESPECIALLY WHETHER HER EYES ARE ALL RIGHT...

STEVE CANYON
by MILTON CANIFF
WHEN DOE REDWOOD CRASHES INTO THE SEA, STEVE, HOLLY AND MR. HALL ARE ABLE TO REACH THE SINKING AIRCRAFT, WHILE THE SUBMARINE RUNS DOWN THE RETREATING RED JUNK...
407
A RESCUE SEAPLANE COMES ALONGSIDE AND TAKES THE PARTY ABOARD
ANY WORD, DOCTOR?
SHE'S UNDER SEDATION! — TOO EARLY TO KNOW HOW BADLY HURT SHE IS...
IMAGINE THAT DARLIN' GIRL DOIN' ALL THAT FOR ME — HER BIG RIVAL!
RIVAL, HOLLY? FOR WHAT?

WHY, DADDY, YOU EMBARRASS ME—ALTHOUGH I RECKON MOST EVERYONE KNOWS BY NOW THAT MISS REDWOOD AND I ARE COMPETING FOR COL. CANYON!
WELL, AH —LOOK HERE NOW, HOLLY —I---
Y'SEE, STEVE, MY DARLIN' DADDY IS A YANKEE! HE'S DISTRESSED AT FACTS OF LIFE LIKE THIS... I MUST HAVE A LONG TALK WITH HIM VERY SOON!
HOWEVER, YOUR DADDY KNOWS A FEW OTHER FACTS THAT HAVE BEEN USEFUL! HOW DO YOU THINK HE GOT YOU RELEASED FROM THE JUNK?
BY PAYIN' 10,000 U.S. DOLLARS--GREAT DAY!! WHERE DID YOU FIND THAT MUCH MONEY, DADDY?
NAVY
COUNTERFEIT U.S. DOLLARS PRODUCED BY THE JAPANESE ARMY ON FORMOSA DURING THE WAR! YOU'RE WORTH MORE THAN THAT TO ME IN REAL MONEY, BABY, BUT THERE'S A TIME AND PLACE FOR EVERYTHING!
MY SHREWD YANKEE DADDY!
MEANWHILE—AT THE U.S. NAVY HOSPITAL...
KIMBERLY, SKIPPER SAYS THE WOMAN STAYS PUT! THE RESCUE PLANE IS ALSO BRINGING HER HUSBAND AND DAUGHTER!
OKAY!
THAT ISN'T THE ONLY REASON MRS. HALL IS HERE—SHE HEARD THE REDWOOD GAL MAY HAVE BEEN BLINDED BY THE CRASH!
Copyright 1955, Field Enterprises, Inc.
4-24

4/25
Registered U.S. Patent Office.
PATIENT'S NAME IS DOE REDWOOD. SICK BAY EMERGENCY IS STANDING BY...
OH, DADDY —WHAT CAN WE DO FOR THAT DOWNRIGHT WONDERFUL WOMAN?
LET THE NAVY HANDLE IT FOR THE MOMENT, HOLLY!
OH! THERE'S MY BEAUTIFUL MOTHER...
MOTHER!
AS MRS. HALL TURNS TOWARD THE SOUND OF HER DAUGHTER'S VOICE SHE DOES SOMETHING BLIND PEOPLE LEARN NEVER TO DO —SHE TAKES AN UNEXPLORED STEP FORWARD...
MILTON CANIFF

4/26
Copyright 1955, Field Enterprises, Inc.
IN HER EAGERNESS TO REACH HOLLY, BLIND MRS. HALL STARTS ACROSS THE DOCK TOWARD THE SOUND OF HER DAUGHTER'S VOICE...
MOTHER! -NO!
MILTON CANIFF
MOTHER! -ARE YOU ALL RIGHT?
WHOEVER YOU ARE —THANKS —I AM SO HORRIBLY EMBARRASSED!

4/27
Copyright 1955, Field Enterprises, Inc. Registered U.S. Patent Office.
MOTHER, DEAR, ARE YOU HURT ?
NO, HOLLY! —THANKS TO THIS YOUNG MAN
KIMBERLY! WHAT'S THE IDEA OF LEAVING YOUR POST?
WE ARE SO VERY GRATE--
GOTTA RUN-
GIL! WHAT HAPPENED? ARE YOU ALL RIGHT?
OH, DADDY, A NICE MARINE CAUGHT HER, BUT HE WAS CALLED BACK— THE GUARD MUST BE CHANGING... THEY'RE GETTING INTO A TRUCK
THE MARINES FELL BACK, BUT FROM THE LOOK ON HOLLY'S FACE I WOULD GUESS THERE'LL BE A COUNTERATTACK VERY SOON...
MILTON CANIFF

4/28
Copyright 1955, Field Enterprises, Inc. Registered U.S. Patent Office.
HOMER, WHAT IS THE WORD ABOUT DOE REDWOOD?
CANYON IS AT THE HOSPITAL —HE SAYS SHE IS HURT, BUT THEY HAVEN'T GIVEN HIM DETAILS
HOW IS OUR HOLLY FEELING AFTER HER ORDEAL?
WHAT A KID! SHE WAS UP AT DAWN AND OVER TO THE HOSPITAL TO SEE DOE REDWOOD...
THAT'S FITTING INDEED... BY THE WAY, HOMER, DID YOU SEE THE MAN WHO KEPT ME FROM FALLING OFF THE DOCK?
HE WAS HARDLY A MAN... MORE OF A BOY! -ABOUT HOLLY'S AGE!
MILTON CANIFF
HE WAS ONE OF THE MARINES STATIONED AT THE HOSPITAL GATE!
MMM-HMMM...

4/29
I NEVER HAVE UNDERSTOOD YOU, KIMBERLY, BUT TRADING DUTY ASSIGNMENTS IS THE END...
WHADYA GOT, ROCKS IN YOUR HEAD OR SOMETHIN', TO WANTA BE STUCK ON THIS HOSPITAL GATE ?... HEY! DIG THIS!
HEL-LO
HELLO!
MILTON CANIFF
I'LL BE BACK
I'LL BE HERE!
I'LL BE... WELL, I'LL JUST BE...
Copyright 1955, Field Enterprises, Inc.
Registered U. S. Patent Office

4/30
THAT YOU, STEVE?
YES, DOE... TAKE IT EASY, BABY...
I'M STRAPPED DOWN — SO I WON'T TOUCH MY FACE — HUH? TOO MUCH GUNSIGHT; BAD FOR THE COMPLEXION!
OH, YOU WERE JUMPING AROUND FOR A WHILE... THESE NAVY DOCS ARE CAUTIOUS CHARACTERS!
MILTON CANIFF
YOU AND HOLLY AND HER FATHER GOT AWAY OKAY ?
YES!
AND THEY ALL LIVED HAPPILY EVER AFTER...
Copyright 1955, Field Enterprises, Inc.
Registered U. S. Patent Office

STEVE CANYON
by MILTON CANIFF
HOLLY, HONEY, IT'S A MERCY TO HAVE YOU BACK HOME! WE MUST HURRY SO WE DON'T MISS THE VISITING HOURS AT THE NAVY HOSPITAL...
OH, I'M READY, MOTHER, DEAR... I'M WEARIN' MY LIGHT BLUE!
YOU CERTAINLY HAVE BEEN CONSCIENTIOUS ABOUT VISITING WITH MISS DOE! —AND RIGHT ON TIME, TOO!
YES, MOTHER, DEAR...
THERE'S SOME CASH MONEY IN MY DESK DRAWER... PLEASE ARRANGE FOR FRESH FLOWERS TO GO TO HER REGULARLY
BUT, MOTHER, DEAR —THAT MONEY WAS FOR THE RECORDINGS OF SHAKESPEARE FOR YOU--
HUSH, HONEY! MISS DOE WAS NEARLY KILLED SAVING YOUR LIFE... IT'S SO FINE THAT SHE IS GOING TO BE ABLE TO SEE THE FLOWERS...
Y-YES, MOTHER, DEAR...

MAY I SEE YOUR PASS, MA'AM!
---THAT VOICE IS SO FAMILIAR! IS THE SAME GUARD ALWAYS ON DUTY HERE?
WHY, NO, MA'AM—IT'S JUST A SORT OF COINCIDENCE
WELL, IF OUR PASS IS IN ORDER, MAY WE GO INSIDE?
OH, YES, MA'AM
HOLLY, THE YOUNG MAN SAYS WE MAY GO IN!
HOLLY, DEAR, ARE YOU THERE?
OH—Y-YES, MOTHER...
HEADS UP!
100
GEE, LADY—I BEG YOUR PARDON—I-I DIDN'T REALIZE...YOU'RE BLIND!
TECHNICALLY, YES... ACTUALLY I THINK I SEE CLEARLY WHAT'S HAPPENING...
5-1

5/2
Copyright 1956, Field Enterprises, Inc. Registered U.S. Patent Office.
MISS DOE, MR. HALL AND I ARE DESPERATE, TRYING TO THINK OF SOME WAY TO MAKE IT UP TO YOU FOR WHAT YOU DID FOR OUR HOLLY...
IT WAS A CALCULATED RISK, MRS. HALL... I FELT GUILTY BECAUSE THE REDS MISTOOK HER FOR ME...
THEY TELL ME YOU AREN'T —AH —THAT YOUR EYES ARE ALL RIGHT...
YES... MY FACE MAY LOOK LIKE SOMETHING FRANKENSTEIN THOUGHT UP, BUT IF I STAY AWAY FROM MIRRORS I WON'T HAVE TO LOOK AT IT!
—MAYBE IT WOULD BE BETTER IF I WERE BLIND!
MILTON CANIFF
OH, I'M SORRY, MRS. HALL! YOU'RE SO GRACIOUS THAT I FORGOT YOU CAN'T SEE! WILL YOU FORGIVE ME?
OF COURSE, MY DEAR! WHEN YOU ARE BLIND YOU'RE EITHER BITTER OR FORGIVING! THERE ARE DAYS WHEN I CAN KEEP THE BITTERNESS ALMOST UNDER CONTROL!

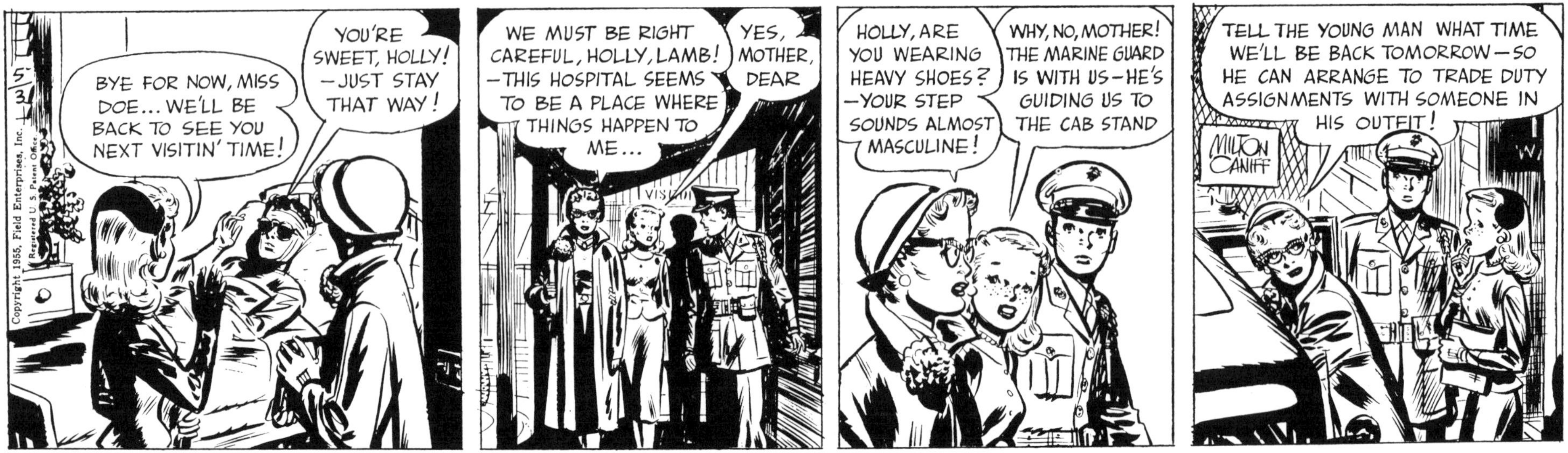
5-3
Copyright 1956, Field Enterprises, Inc. Registered U.S. Patent Office.
BYE FOR NOW, MISS DOE... WE'LL BE BACK TO SEE YOU NEXT VISITIN' TIME!
YOU'RE SWEET, HOLLY! —JUST STAY THAT WAY!
WE MUST BE RIGHT CAREFUL, HOLLY, LAMB! —THIS HOSPITAL SEEMS TO BE A PLACE WHERE THINGS HAPPEN TO ME...
YES, MOTHER, DEAR
HOLLY, ARE YOU WEARING HEAVY SHOES? —YOUR STEP SOUNDS ALMOST MASCULINE!
WHY, NO, MOTHER! THE MARINE GUARD IS WITH US—HE'S GUIDING US TO THE CAB STAND
TELL THE YOUNG MAN WHAT TIME WE'LL BE BACK TOMORROW—SO HE CAN ARRANGE TO TRADE DUTY ASSIGNMENTS WITH SOMEONE IN HIS OUTFIT!
MILTON CANIFF

5/4
Copyright 1955, Field Enterprises, Inc.
Registered U.S. Patent Office
WHEN YOUR HEART'S ON ♪ FIRE...♫
AH, SWEET MYSTERY OF LIFE...♫ ♫
FROM THE HALLS ♪ OF MONTEZUMA... ♫ ♫
HELLO, STEVE, THIS IS GILBERTA HALL...I HAVE A PROBLEM
MILTON CANIFF

5/5
Copyright 1955, Field Enterprises, Inc.
Registered U.S. Patent Office
WHY, HELLO, GIL...
STEVE, I HAVE A FAVOR TO ASK! -I WONDER IF YOU COULD---
LATER
CAPTAIN, WHO COMMANDS THE MARINE DE-TACHMENT AT THE NAVY HOSPITAL PIER?
LIEUTENANT HELLMAN, SIR!
LIEUTENANT HELLMAN, THIS IS LT. COL. CANYON, AIR FORCE...I WONDER IF YOU COULD DO ME A FAVOR--
GLAD TO TRY, SIR
MILTON CANIFF
GUNNY, THIS IS LIEUT. HELLMAN! I HAVE SOMETHING I WANT YOU TO DO...
WOTS ON THE LOOTENINT'S MIND, SIR?...

5/6
Copyright 1955, Field Enterprises, Inc. Registered U. S. Patent Office.
AWRITE — I WANT A VOLUNTEER T'BE A BABY-SITTER AT THE YOO-ESS CONSULATE!
IF THE BABY'S OVER 18, I'LL MAKE TH' NOBLE SACRIFICE!
KIMBERLY, YOU BEEN TRADIN' DUTY ASSIGNMENTS LIKE A SEA LAWYER SO'S YOU COULD CASE THAT PIGEON WHO COMES TO THE HOSPITAL...
A TOUR OF BABY-SITTIN' MAY TEACH YOU TH PITFALLS OF LOVE... I RECKON YOU JUST NOW VOLUNTEERED!
MILTON CANIFF

5/7
Copyright 1955, Field Enterprises, Inc. Registered U. S. Patent Office.
WELL, KIMBERLY, Y' OUGHTA BE GLAD Y' PULLED A TOUR AS A BABY-SITTER — YOU CAN PUT IN FOR ORDNANCE AN' QUALIFY AS A POWDER EXPERT!
LOOK ALIVE THERE, REED, BOY — IT WOULD BE AWFUL IF A RED SPY BROKE IN DURING YOUR WATCH AN' STOLE THE 'FORMULA' FROM THE U.S. CONSULATE!
MEANWHILE...
COME IN, STEVE! —ANY WORD ABOUT DOE REDWOOD?
HER COMPANY HAS A PLASTIC SURGEON ENGAGED STATESIDE TO WORK ON HER FACE... THE NAVY WILL FLY HER HOME!
MILTON CANIFF
GIL, DOES HOLLY KNOW STEVE IS HERE? SHE'LL WANT TO HURRY DOWN TO SAY HELLO!
THE CHILD HAS BEEN SIGHING AND CARRYING ON ALL WEEK, STEVE! I SURELY HOPE SOMETHING CAN BE DONE TO BREAK HER MOOD!
I'M CERTAIN THERE'S A SOLUTION FOR WHAT AILS HOLLY!

STEVE CANYON
by MILTON CANIFF
THE NAVY IS FLYING DOE REDWOOD BACK TO THE STATES... HER COMPANY WANTS HER TREATED BY THEIR OWN DOCTORS...
STEVE, WHAT CAN WE EVER DO TO SHOW HER OUR GRATITUDE?
BUT I'M WORRIED ABOUT HOLLY... SINCE THE KIDNAPPING SHE SEEMS TO BE IN A KIND OF DAZE...
PRETTY ROUGH DEAL FOR A YOUNG LADY, MR. HALL...
YES, BUT SHE WAS ALL RIGHT FOR A FEW DAYS... THEN IT BEGAN! —SHE EVEN LOST HER APPETITE... WHICH IS MOST UNUSUAL...
REALLY? I'M SORRY TO HEAR THAT
MIST' HALL, IS YOUNG U.S. MILITARY BY FRONT DOOR!
THAT'S ODD... I DIDN'T SEND FOR ANYONE...

I AM HOMER HALL— DID YOU WISH TO SEE ME, SON ?
YOU'RE MIS-TER HALL? GEE—I WAS JUST TOLD TO REPORT TO THE CONSULATE, SIR! ARE YOU THE MISTER HALL? HER FATHER?
WE'LL—THIS IS OBVIOUSLY NOT FOR ME! NAMU, PLEASE CALL MISS HO---
I DO DECLARE, FATHER...I WAS JUST PASSIN' BY... WHAT A RARE COINCIDENCE!
I TAKE IT THAT YOU TWO ALREADY KNOW EACH OTHER! WHAT IS YOUR NAME, MY BOY?
KIM REEDERLY, CLIVATE PIRST FLASS! I MEAN REED KIMBERLY, PRIVATE FIRST CLASS, SIR!
WELL, NOW THAT YOU'RE HERE YOU ARE WELCOME, KIMBERLY...
THANK YOU, SIR...
BUT I STILL CAN'T UNDERSTAND HOW YOU WERE ORDERED TO REPORT HERE!
IT MUST HAVE BEEN SOME REAL INTELLIGENT OFFICER WHO JUS' KNEW THE U.S. CONSULATE NEEDED A BIG MARINE TO GUARD OUR INTERESTS
Copyright 1955, Field Enterprises, Inc.
5-8

5/9
Copyright 1955, Field Enterprises, Inc. Registered U.S. Patent Office.
WHO WAS IT, HOMER, DEAR ?
STRANGEST THING... IT'S A YOUNG MARINE WHO SAID HE WAS TOLD TO REPORT TO THE CONSULATE...AND HAD THE ORDERS TO PROVE IT...
DO YOU KNOW ANYTHING ABOUT THIS, STEVE ?
YES! HOLLY MET YOUNG KIMBERLY AT THE NAVY HOSPITAL, BUT IT'S HARD TO SNAG A PASS THESE DAYS —SO I PULLED A LITTLE INSIDE JOB AND GOT HIM SPRUNG FOR THE EVENING!
MILTON CANIFF
WITHOUT KNOWING ANY FURTHER DETAILS, I AM CONVINCED THAT SOMEHOW, SOMEWHICH WAY, MY SPHINX-LIKE BRIDE SET UP THE ENTIRE THING!

5/10
Copyright 1955, Field Enterprises, Inc. Registered U.S. Patent Office.
I DECLARE — IT'S SUCH A MERCY THAT THE MARINE CORPS HAD THE GOOD JUDGMENT TO SEND A MAN OVER HERE TO THE CONSULATE
MY, BUT THAT'S A PRETTY NAME YOU HAVE, PRIVATE KIMBERLY! MAKES ME THINK OF DIAMONDS!
'FRAID THAT'S AS CLOSE AS I'LL EVER COME TO BEING RICH!
BUT THERE ARE LOADS OF OTHER DESIRABLE THINGS IN LIFE! WANT TO HEAR SOME RECORDS?
MILTON CANIFF
HOMER, DO YOU RECKON HOLLY AND HER BEAU ARE GETTING ACQUAINTED?
THEY JUST SWITCHED FROM TURK MURPHY TO FRED WARING, SO I THINK THEY'RE BREAKING DOWN THE SOCIAL BARRIERS!

5/11
Copyright 1955, Field Enterprises, Inc.
GLORY BE, REED! IT'S SUCH A MERCY TO FIND A BOY WHO DANCES WELL!
'GEE, MISS HOLLY, IF A GUY COULDN'T DANCE WITH YOU, THEN HIS FEET MUST BE ON BACKWARDS
MILTON CANIFF
...YOU SAY SUCH PRETTY THINGS—I DON'T KNOW HOW I WAS ABLE TO GET YOU AWAY FROM ALL THE OTHER GIRLS FOR AN EVENING!
I KNOW HOW SWEET YOU SOUTHERN GIRLS CAN TALK, BUT WE BOTH REALIZE THERE ARE ALMOST NO OTHER GIRLS ON THIS ROCK!
IF YOU YANKEE BOYS DIDN'T GO ANALYZIN' THINGS ALL THE TIME YOU WOULDN'T HAVE GOT US SO TUCKERED OUT WE HAD TO REST A SPELL AT APPOMATTOX!
I HAVE TO GET GOING, FOLKS... I WANT TO SAY HELLO TO REED KIMBERLY ON THE WAY...
OH, YOU KNOW THE BOY, STEVE?
WHY, HOMER, YOU JUST KNOW STEVE WOULDN'T HAVE FIXED IT FOR THAT LAD TO COME SEE HOLLY UNLESS HE WAS CERTAIN TO BE RIGHT FOR OUR GIRL!

5/12
Copyright 1955, Field Enterprises, Inc. Registered U. S. Patent Office.
KNOCK! KNOCK! I'M LEAVING, SO I'D LIKE TO SAY GOOD NIGHT TO THE GUEST OF HONOR!
W-WHY, IT'S STEVE CANYON! —HOLLY, WHY DIDN'T YOU TELL ME HE WAS HERE?
MILTON CANIFF
WELL, I--
THE BIG TIMES WE USED TO HAVE!
WHAT ARE YOU DOING, NOW, STEVE? I'M IN THE MARINES
I RECKON COLONEL CANYON CAN SEE THAT, REED!
COLONEL CANYON? GEE, SIR, I DIDN'T KNOW, SIR! NO, SIR! I DIDN'T KNOW, SIR!—OR DID I SAY THAT, SIR?—WOW, SIR!

5/13
Copyright 1955, Field Enterprises, Inc. Registered U. S. Patent Office
GOOD NIGHT, COLONEL CANYON, SIR! PLEASANT DREAMS, SIR! —YES, SIR!
WHY, REED KIMBERLY— I DECLARE YOU SOUNDED LIKE A DRUMMER BOY TALKIN' TO NAPOLEON! STEVE CANYON IS JUST A PLAIN OL' LIEUTENANT COLONEL IN THE AIR FORCE!
WHY, I NEVER MET A COLONEL BEFORE, MISS HOLLY! WHEN YOU'VE BEEN THROUGH MARINE CORPS BOOT TRAINING, A GUNNERY SERGEANT LOOKS LIKE A FOUR-STAR GENERAL!
MILTON CANIFF
WHY, OF COURSE, REED — I RECKON US SILLY OL' GIRLS JUS' DON'T UNDER-STAND THESE MILITARY MATTERS
I'LL BET YOU WERE THE VERY BEST BOOT IN CAMP!
WELL, AS A MATTER OF FACT, I DID DO FAIRLY WELL AT GOOD OLD PARRIS ISLAND...

5/14
Copyright 1955, Field Enterprises, Inc. Registered U. S. Patent Office
GEE, MISS HOLLY, YOU ARE NICE TO LISTEN TO ME TELL ABOUT THE MARINE CORPS...
ACTUALLY, I'M ALWAYS BEING KIDDED BY THE GUYS IN MY OUTFIT!
WHY IN THE WIDE WORLD WOULD THEY HAVE REASON TO POKE FUN AT YOU, REED?
OH—BECAUSE I DON'T HAVE A GIRL THAT IS—I—WELL—
MILTON CANIFF
I DO DECLARE, YOU MUST HAVE KEPT YOUR SECRET WELL FROM THOSE MARINES! A GIRL KNOWS RIGHT AWAY WHEN A BOY HAS A STRING OF PRETTIES PININ' AWAY FOR HIM BACK HOME! SHAME ON YOU!

STEVE CANYON
MILTON CANIFF
HOLLY!
YES, REED?
MAYBE YOU THINK THAT I'M A PRETTY ROUGH CHARACTER, BEING A MARINE AND ALL!
WHY I-I THINK YOU ARE JUST ROUGH ENOUGH, REED!
I GUESS YOU'D BE ANGRY IF I KISSED YOU!
W-WHY, I DON'T RIGHTLY KNOW..

HOLLY, HONEY, IS THAT YOU ?
YES, MOTHER!
I THOUGHT REED WAS WITH YOU !
HE WAS—BUT HE KISSED ME ON THE CHEEK, THEN RAN AWAY!.. I AM WORRIED, MOTHER...
WHY, DEAR — A LITTLE SHYNESS IS RIGHT BECOMING IN A YOUNG MAN THESE DAYS !
OH THAT DOESN'T BOTHER ME — BUT HOW AM I GOING TO TELL STEVE CANYON THAT IT'S ALL OVER BETWEEN US ?
Copyright 1955, Field Enterprises, Inc. 5-15

5/16
Copyright 1955, Field Enterprises, Inc. Registered U.S. Patent Office.
KIMBERLY, Y'GOT ANY SAFETY PINS LEFT OVER FROM THE HOLD-UP?
AS YOUNG AS YOU ACT, I'LL BET YOU HAD NO SWEAT MAKIN' TALK WITH THAT BABY YOU SAT WITH...
DIDJA GET A PITCHA OF LI'L SNOOKUMS T' CARRY IN Y' WALLET?
YEAH—TO REMIND YOU OF YOUR BIG ADVENTURE
SURE! -I GOT ONE...
MILTON CANIFF
WANNA FLIP TO SEE WHICH KICKS WHICH FIRST?

5/17
Copyright 1955, Field Enterprises, Inc. Registered U.S. Patent Office.
THIS IS WAR-WARY FORMOSA—AND, AS EVERYBODY KNOWS, A MARINE AND HIS GIRL COULD NOT FIND A CHANCE TO GET TOGETHER...
...HE IS RESTRICTED TO HIS BASE MOST OF THE TIME...
AND EVEN WHEN HE HAS A PASS, THE PRICES ARE TOO HIGH FOR HIM TO TAKE HER ANYWHERE
THERE IS COMPETITION FROM THE OFFICERS AS WELL AS OTHER ENLISTED MEN
...SO IT IS PERFECTLY OBVIOUS THAT, LACKING THE USUAL AIDS TO YOUNG LOVERS, HOLLY HALL AND P.F.C. REED KIMBERLY COULD NOT POSSIBLY HAVE BECOME SWEETHEARTS
MILTON CANIFF

5/18
Copyright 1955, Field Enterprises, Inc.
Registered U. S. Patent Office.
DON'T BLOW YOUR STACK, KIMBERLY! —WE'RE JUST HANGIN' AROUND IN CASE YOU MIGHTA BUSTED A LEG ON YOUR WAY TO KEEP YOUR DATE WITH HOLLY HALL!
MILTON CANIFF

5/19
Copyright 1955, Field Enterprises, Inc
Registered U. S. Patent Office.
HOLLY—IT'S GOT TO BE EITHER STEVE CANYON OR ME!
WHY, REED, I DECLARE—I NEVER IN MY WHOLE LIFE HEARD OF SUCH A THING!..THERE'S ABSOLUTELY NO COMPARISON BETWEEN YOU AND COL. CANYON!
THERE SURE ISN'T! HE'S A LIEUTENANT COLONEL IN THE AIR FORCE, AND I'M JUST ONE STRIPE NORTH OF A BOOT MARINE...
GREAT DAY, REED, YOU TOLD ME YOURSELF THAT A MARINE PRIVATE WAS A BETTER MAN THAN A FOUR-STAR OFFICER IN THE OTHER BRANCHES
I RECKON YOU WERE JUST SAYIN' WHAT YOU SAID SO I WOULDN'T THINK YOU WERE BRAGGIN' AN' GLOATIN' OVER YOUR OLD FRIEND STEVE CANYON!
WELL—AH—I HADN'T THOUGHT OF IT THAT WAY... MAYBE YOU'RE RIGHT...
MILTON CANIFF

5/20
Copyright 1955, Field Enterprises, Inc.
Registered U.S. Patent Office.
YOU GAVE THAT KIMBERLY KID ANOTHER PASS? ... HE GETS MORE SHORE TIME THAN THE ADMIRAL!
MARINE CORPS PUBLIC RELATIONS, MATE! HE'S THE ONLY MAN IN THE OUTFIT WHO'S FOUND A GAL TO HAVE DATES WITH!
KID, IF THAT PIGEON COOS TOO COZY, SEND FOR ME!
DON'T LET HIM SNOW YOU, REED! GALS WHO GO OUT WITH THAT MARINE ASK FOR REFUNDS ON THEIR INCOME TAXES!
LOOKS AS IF THE BABYFACE HAS THAT HALL CHICK YELLING 'SEMPER FIDELIS'!
MAYBE, BUT I JUST NOW SAW HER GET INTO A TAXI IN TOWN WITH THAT AIR FORCE COLONEL CANYON!
MILTON CANIFF

5/21
Copyright 1955, Field Enterprises, Inc.
Registered U.S. Patent Office.
U.S. COAST GUARD
MILTON CANIFF
CORDON SANITAIRE 1955
...THAT'S JUST A FANCY PHRASE FOR THE BIG 'KEEP OUT' SIGN THAT THE PEOPLE IN UNIFORM REPRESENT TO ANYBODY WHO MIGHT WANT TO UPSET THIS WAY OF LIFE WE CHERISH...
...IT'S NO YACHTING PARTY FOR THE KID FREEZING HIS EARS ON THE DECK WATCH OF A DESTROYER IN THE 7th FLEET, AND IT IS NO HEIDELBERG BEER BINGE FOR THE DOGFACE ON BORDER PATROL IN GERMANY...
...WHEN YOU'RE WORKING IN YOUR GARDEN—REMEMBER THAT YOU'LL LIVE TO SEE THE SEEDS BEAR FRUIT OR FLOWERS BECAUSE THE RING OF STEEL AROUND YOU IS WELDED BY LIVING FLESH!
...THIS IS ARMED FORCES DAY!

STEVE CANYON
by MILTON CANIFF
SMALL STORES
W-WHY, IT'S HOLLY— AND COL. CANYON! I ---

COLONEL CANYON, SIR!
HEY- IT'S REED!
WHY, REED, HONEY-I-
COLONEL, I KNOW WHAT IT MAY MEAN FOR ME TO SAY THIS, BUT IF YOU WANT TO TRY TO STEAL MY GIRL YOU'LL HAVE TO FIGHT ME FIRST!
OH, REED! -YOU DON'T KN--
WAIT, HOLLY! GO ON, PRIVATE KIMBERLY!
WELL-AH, THAT'S ALL, SIR! ARE YOU READY, SIR?
HOLLY, DO YOU REALIZE THAT THIS MAN IS RISKING A PRISON SENTENCE TO EVEN THREATEN TO STRIKE AN OFFICER?
Y-YES
THEN WE'D BETTER TELL HIM THAT YOU MADE AN APPOINTMENT WITH ME TO SAY THAT OUR ROMANCE WAS OFF BECAUSE... YOU HAD FALLEN IN LOVE WITH REED KIMBERLY- THEN YOU KISSED ME GOODBYE TO SHOW WE WERE STILL FRIENDS...
FROM THE HALLS OF MON-TAY-ZOO-OO-MUH--
Copyright 1955, Field Enterprises, Inc.
5-22

5/23
REED KIMBERLY, I DON'T RIGHTLY KNOW WHAT TO DO ABOUT YOU!
IT WAS COL. CANYON WHO ARRANGED FOR US TO MEET— YET YOU JUST NOW THREATENED TO HIT HIM...
Copyright 1955, Field Enterprises, Inc. Registered U. S. Patent Office.
BUT HE WAS KISSING YOU, HOLLY! OH, GOLLY, I'M SO MISERABLE!
HE WAS KISSING ME GOODBYE BECAUSE I TOLD HIM I'M—WELL —AH—IN LOVE WITH YOU!
YOU ARE ?
YOU SAID IT RIGHT OUT LOUD!
THOUGHT FOR A MINUTE WE HAD A CUSTOMER!
Y'NEVER KNOW... SOME WIMMIN JUS' NATURALLY LIKE TO BE HOLLERED AT!
SP
MILTON CANIFF

5/24
OH, HOLLY, I I-I-
DON'T TRY TO TALK, REED, HONEY...
Copyright 1955, Field Enterprises, Inc. Registered U. S. Patent Office.
Y'JUST MADE IT, MAC! Y'SEEM T'BE MIGHTY HAPPY...
GUESS YOU GOT THE SCOOP! —WE'RE SHOVIN' OFF OUTA THIS LOUSY LIBERTY PORT!
?!!!?
MILTON CANIFF

5/25
Copyright 1955, Field Enterprises, Inc. Registered U. S. Patent Office.
HAVE YOU SLIPPED Y' CABLE, KIMBERLY? WE'RE SHOVIN' OUTA THIS PARRY-DIZE OF THE PACIFIC! YOU GET NO PASS TO NO PLACE!
OHH-H-H
BUT, SARGE —I —MY GIRL...THAT IS...
THE SOBBIN' LOCKER IS AFT, GYRENE! THE CHAPLAIN IS WAITIN' T' HEAR YORE TOUCHIN' TALE!
HOLLY, WE'RE SHOVING OFF! —I HAVE TO SEE YOU —I CAN'T GET A PASS, BUT I'LL MEET YOU AT THE BLUE CAT RESTAURANT IN THE OLD CITY...
OH, REED —I'M NOT SUPPOSED TO GO OUT ALONE AT NIGHT... B-BUT I'LL BE THERE...
MILTON CANIFF

5/26
Copyright 1955, Field Enterprises, Inc. Registered U. S. Patent Office.
I-I'D LIKE A BOOTH WHERE MY GIRL AND I CAN HAVE SOME PRIVACY...
BUT OF COURSE, HONORED MILITARY! —AND THE -AH- LADY?
SHE'LL ASK FOR ME WHEN SHE ARRIVES... I'M PRIVATE W.T. DOOR!
AH, SO!
MEANWHILE...
MOTHER, I RECKON I'LL GO TO MY ROOM AND STUDY!
ALL RIGHT, HOLLY, PET!
BUT HOLLY DOESN'T GO TO HER ROOM... KNOWING HER MOTHER WILL NOT DISTURB HER 'STUDYING', SHE LEAVES BY THE SIDE DOOR... HOWEVER, THERE ARE FLAWS IN HER PLAN...
MILTON CANIFF

5/27
Copyright 1955, Field Enterprises, Inc. Registered U.S. Patent Office
WELL, CANYON, I GUESS THIS WAS INEVITABLE... WE HAVE A TIP THAT THE BLACK MARKET MOB IS TRYING TO PEDDLE POLIO VACCINE OUT HERE!
PROBABLY CUTTING IT AS THEY DID PENICILLIN! —SOME INNOCENT PEOPLE WILL NEVER KNOW WHAT HIT THEM...
THE NAVY HOSPITAL HAS SOME SERUM FOR MILITARY DEPENDENTS, BUT THE SCOOP SAYS THIS STUFF MIGHT BE COMING FROM STATESIDE BY AIR—WHICH PUTS IT IN OUR LAPS...
MILTON CANIFF
THE TIP SAYS A CONTACT WITH THE LOCAL BUYERS FOR THE CHINESE REDS IS DUE TO BE SET UP AT THE BLUE CAT CAFE... WE'LL SEAL OFF THE JOINT AND PULL A FULL-SCALE RAID—AND SEE WHAT WE COME UP WITH...
—WITH REED ALREADY THERE AND HOLLY ON HER WAY, IT SEEMS CERTAIN THAT THE POLICE WILL COME UP WITH SOMETHING...

5/28
Copyright 1955, Field Enterprises, Inc. Registered U.S. Patent Office
GIL, THIS IS HOMER... GOT TO FLY TO JAPAN ON AN EMERGENCY THING... I HATE TO HAVE TO---
NOW, HOMER, HONEY, DON'T YOU FRET FOR ONE MINUTE! HOLLY AND I ARE SNUG AND SECURE—AND NAMU WILL LOOK AFTER US...
YOU HURRY BACK, DO YOU HEAR?
MILTON CANIFF
THE SERVANT HAS SEEN HOLLY LEAVE THE HOUSE —SHOULD HE TELL MRS. HALL OR REMAIN THE SILENT ASIATIC?
MEANWHILE, REED KIMBERLY WAITS IMPATIENTLY FOR HOLLY IN A BOOTH AT THE BLUE CAT CAFE...WHILE CERTAIN OTHER ACTIVITIES ARE TAKING PLACE IN THE NEXT CUBICLE...

STEVE CANYON
by MILTON CANIFF
NAMU, MR. HALL HAS BEEN CALLED TO AN EMERGENCY MEETING IN JAPAN ... WILL YOU TELL MISS HOLLY THAT I WISH TO SEE HER?.. SHE'S IN HER ROOM, STUDYING ...
AH – UH – MISSY HOLLY NOT SO IN ROOM!
SOON TIME AGO SHE LEAVE ALONE BY SIDE DOOR! NAMU NOT CARRY TALE, MA'AM— BUT YOU ASK!
HOLLY KNOWS SHE MUSTN'T BE ALONE IN THE CITY STREETS AFTER DARK! NAMU, PLEASE GO FIND HER ...
BUT THIS WILL LEAVE MA'AM ALONE IN HOUSE! MIST' HALL SAY THIS MUS'NOT DO EVER!
IT'S MUCH MORE IMPORTANT TO FIND HOLLY!— GO! HURRY!
MEANWHILE = IN A NATIVE CAFE ...
WHO, THEN, IS THE LONE YANKEE MILITARY OF SUCH HUMBLE RANK?
HE DESIRED A CURTAINED AREA WHEREIN TO DINE HIS LOVE— AND PRODUCED A TIP IN KEEPING WITH HIS REQUEST ...

YOU ORDER MAYBE? MUCH TIME GO 'WAY ON CLOCK!
MY GIRL WILL BE HERE!..MY OUTFIT'S GOING TO MOVE! I'VE GOT TO SEE HER! —SHE'S A PRETTY BLONDE!
NO GIRL ASK FOR 'PLIVATE W.T. DOOR' —LIKE YOU SAY WILL DO...
PLENTY CUSTOMER TONIGHT! —MANY WANT PLIVATE PLACES LIKE THIS...
HERE'S SOME MORE STALLING MONEY— SHE'S SURE TO BE ALONG SOON!
別動
FOR THOSE OF YOU WHO SPEAK ENGLISH— —THIS IS A POLICE RAID! DO AS YOU'RE TOLD AND YOU WON'T BE HURT!
THE GOVERNMENT POLICE WILL SEARCH THE MEN...POLICEWOMEN WILL SEARCH THE WOMEN! AMERICAN MILITARY PERSONNEL FALL IN ON THE FAR WALL...
OO-H-H-H – AND I DON'T HAVE A PASS!
AS REED LOOKS ABOUT DESPERATELY FOR A WAY OUT — A HAND SLIPS SOMETHING INSIDE THE CROWN OF HIS CAP...
Copyright 1955, Field Enterprises, Inc.
5-29

5/30
WHERE'S KIMBERLY?
MUST HAVE GONE A.W.O.L. TO SEE HIS GIRL WHEN HE HEARD WE WERE SHOVING OFF!
Copyright 1955, Field Enterprises, Inc. Registered U.S. Patent Office.
MEANWHILE - IN THE OLD SECTION OF THE CITY...
HEY! WHOTSA IDEA, SAILOR? - WANTA GO TO THE BLUE CAT...
NOT TONIGHT, MATE! KEEP MOVING!
MILTON CANIFF
AND INSIDE.
HEY, GYRENE! ALONG THE BACK WALL WITH THE REST OF THE U.S. MILITARY PERSONNEL!
SHOW YOUR PASS TO TOWN AS YOU LINE UP TO BE SEARCHED!
REED HAS NO PASS... AND AT THIS LOW MOMENT, HOLLY ARRIVES AT THE BLUE CAT — WHEREUPON...
I TOLD YOU TO MOVE ON, MATE!
......SHE BLITHELY WALKS INSIDE AS THE SHORE PATROLMAN TURNS AWAY...

5/31
Copyright 1955, Field Enterprises, Inc. Registered U.S. Patent Office.
SHOW YOUR PASS, GYRENE!
SAY, AH-SAILOR, I LEFT MY CAP IN THE BOOTH - I-I--
HOLD YOUR PLACE, MAC! — HEY, TINK! BRING THE MARINE'S CAP FROM THE BOOTH!
NOW—YOUR PASS, MAC
I-AH MUST HAVE LOST MY PASS
HERE'S YOUR CAP!
AS THE THROWN CAP LANDS AT REED KIMBERLY'S FEET, A SMALL VIAL ROLLS OUT FROM INSIDE THE CROWN...
MILTON CANIFF

6/1
Copyright 1955, Field Enterprises, Inc.
Registered U.S. Patent Office
LOOKS AS IF WE HIT THE JACKPOT!
THIS HERE MARINE IS A.W.O.L. FROM THE NAVAL HOSPITAL GUARD —AND HE HAD THE BLACK MARKET POLIO VACCINE IN THE CROWN OF HIS CAP!
NO! NO! I--I--
STOW IT, MAC...
O-O-H-H! REED!
RUN, HONEY! RUN!
MILTON CANIFF

6/2
Copyright 1955, Field Enterprises, Inc.
Registered U.S. Patent Office
THE MARINE WITH THE BLACK MARKET POLIO VACCINE HAD A GIRL FRIEND! SHE RAN OUT THIS DOOR!
MAKE KNOTS, MATE! WE'LL GRAB A STRIPE IF WE WRAP THIS ONE UP!
THE EXIT IS CLEAR FOR A MOMENT AS THE SHORE PATROL SEARCHES THE BACK ROOMS OF THE CAFE... HOLLY MAKES A BREAK FOR THE DOOR—
—BUT HER PURSE CATCHES ON SOME-THING AND SPILLS ITS CONTENTS OVER THE FLOOR...
MILTON CANIFF

6/3
Copyright 1955, Field Enterprises, Inc. Registered U.S. Patent Office
OH, LAWSY
HOLLY HALL DESPERATELY GATHERS THE CONTENTS OF HER SPILLED PURSE...
...THEN AGAIN STARTS FOR THE SIDE EXIT OF THE CAFE — AS THE SHORE PATROL SWINGS AROUND THE CORNER...
HEY! DID YOU SEE A BLONDE GIRL COME OUT OF HERE?
DID SO! DID SO! SHE RUN DOWN STREET TOWARD HARBOR!
NAMU! OH — I'M SO GLAD TO SEE YOU!
THEY GO, MISSY! YOU COME NOW HOMESIDE BEFORE YOU MAMA GET BROKE HEART LIKE SHE NOW GOT BROKE EYES!
MILTON CANIFF

6/4
Copyright 1955, Field Enterprises, Inc. Registered U.S. Patent Office
THE DAME GOT AWAY, BUT HE'LL TELL US WHO IT WAS—WON'T YOU, GYRENE?
WON'T YOU?
U.S.NA
WELL, THIS IS THE FIRST SILENT MARINE I EVER MET!...
BETTER GET HIM TO THE BRIG BEFORE THE OTHER GYRENES FIND OUT ONE OF THEIR GUYS WAS BLACK-MARKETING POLIO VACCINE!
SP
SHORE PATROL
COL. CANYON, WE'RE BOOKING A MARINE P.F.C. NAMED REED KIMBERLY ON THAT VACCINE CASE—I---
HELLO, COL. CANYON!.. ..WHY, HE'S GONE!
INSPECTOR, THE SHORE PATROL HAS A SUSPECT IN THE VACCINE CASE —ONE OF OUR MILITARY PERSONNEL! WILL YOU LET US HANDLE THE WHOLE CASE FROM THIS POINT?
WILL COOPERATE, OF COURSE —JUST AS YANKEE POLICE WOULD DO IF POSITIONS WERE REVERSED— AND THIS WERE U.S.A. INSTEAD OF ASIA!
MILTON CANIFF

STEVE CANYON
by MILTON CANIFF
HERE'S OUR MAN! HE HAD THE BLACK MARKET POLIO SERUM IN THE CROWN OF HIS CAP!
HE'S A.W.O.L. FROM THE MARINE DE-TACHMENT AT THE NAVY HOSPITAL!
HE CHECKS OUT AS P.F.C. REED KIMBERLY!
LISTEN, I --
SP
P
IT FIGURES! WE HAD A TIP THAT THE LOCAL CONTACT WAS IN THAT RES-TAURANT, BUT I NEVER EXPECTED IT TO BE AN AMERICAN MARINE!...
LOOK, PLEASE--
SP
WHAT HAPPENED TO THE BLONDE BABE WHO BLEW IN RIGHT IN THE MIDST OF THE RAID?
SHE BEAT IT!
OH, THANK HEAVEN —HOLLY GOT AWAY!
MEANWHILE...
ALL BE RIGHT NOW, MISSIE HOLLY! SOON HOME!
OH, NAMU, I WAS SO GLAD TO SEE YOU!

MEBBE MISSY HOLLY MAMA DO NOT KNOW 'BOUT SHE GO'WAY!... MEBBE MAMA SLEEPING...
MEBBE MISSY HOLLY JUS' RETIRE QUIET TO BED AN' NEVER GO OUT ALONE AT NIGHT SOME MORE, YES?
YES
MIZ HALL — NAMU THIS SIDE!
COME IN!
MISSY HOLLY NOW SAFE BACK HOME! PLENTY SCARED, BUT NO MISHAP!
SHE THINK MAMA DO NOT KNOW! IF NAMU MIGHT SUGGEST—BEST TO LEAVE SAME SO!
PERHAPS YOU'RE RIGHT...
LISTEN! THE FRONT DOOR-BELL!
WHO IN THE WORLD AT THIS HOUR?
NAVY SHORE PATROL... WE'D LIKE TO TALK TO MISS HOLLISTER HALL...
...SHE MUST HAVE DROPPED HER PURSE IN A PLACE DOWNTOWN — AND THIS IDENTITY CARD FELL OUT! CALL HER, PLEASE!
Copyright 1955, Field Enterprises, Inc.
6-5

6/6
Copyright 1955, Field Enterprises, Inc.
Registered U. S. Patent Office
DON'T KNOW 'BOUT WHAT YOU SAY!
DON'T GIVE US ANY TROUBLE OR WE'LL CALL IN THE LOCAL COPS AND YOU'LL BE IN A SQUEEZE!
WE FOUND THIS IDENTIFICATION CARD DOWNTOWN—IT BELONGS TO MISS HOLLISTER HALL AND GIVES THIS ADDRESS! CALL HER!
I'M LIEUT. COL. CANYON, AIR FORCE... THEY TOLD ME YOU MEN WHO COVERED THE BLUE CAT CAFE WERE HEADED FOR HERE! WANT TO FILL ME IN?
...SO KIMBERLY WAS MEETING A BLONDE DAME, SIR, WE GOT A FLASH OF HER, BUT SHE DUCKED! —THEN WE FOUND THE CARD AND STARTED TO CHECK IT OUT!
NICE GOING! NOW WE'LL PHONE YOUR BOSS AND TELL HIM I'LL TAKE OVER FROM HERE!
MILTON CANIFF

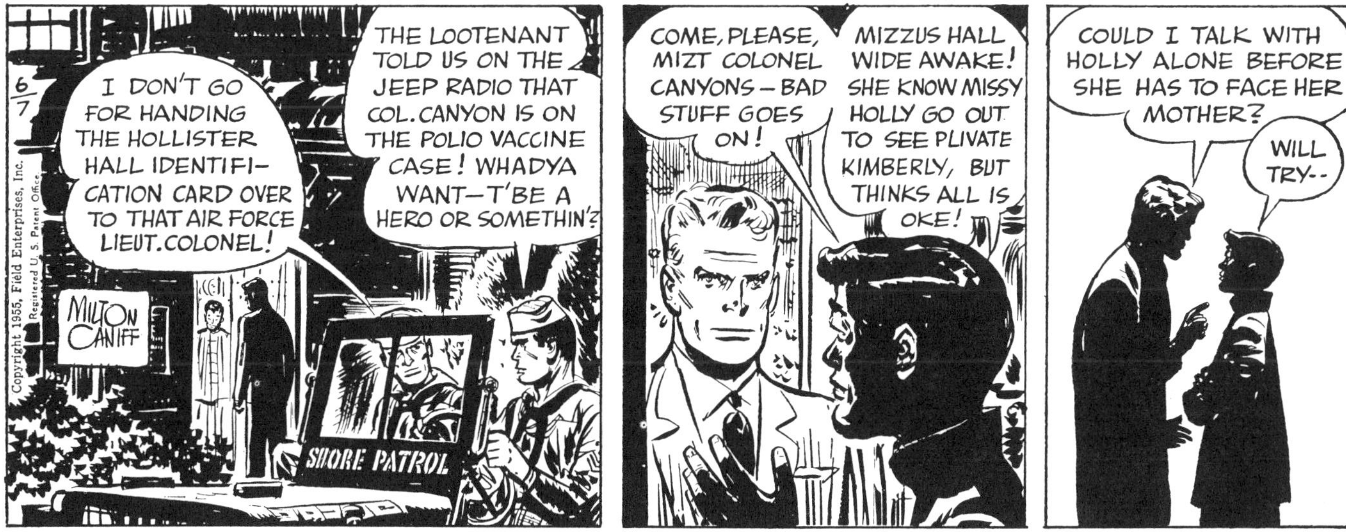
6/7
Copyright 1955, Field Enterprises, Inc.
Registered U. S. Patent Office
I DON'T GO FOR HANDING THE HOLLISTER HALL IDENTIFICATION CARD OVER TO THAT AIR FORCE LIEUT. COLONEL!
THE LOOTENANT TOLD US ON THE JEEP RADIO THAT COL. CANYON IS ON THE POLIO VACCINE CASE! WHADYA WANT—T'BE A HERO OR SOMETHIN'?
MILTON CANIFF
SHORE PATROL
COME, PLEASE, MIZT COLONEL CANYONS—BAD STUFF GOES ON!
MIZZUS HALL WIDE AWAKE! SHE KNOW MISSY HOLLY GO OUT TO SEE PLIVATE KIMBERLY, BUT THINKS ALL IS OKE!
COULD I TALK WITH HOLLY ALONE BEFORE SHE HAS TO FACE HER MOTHER?
WILL TRY--
ONE RATHER SHODDY ASPECT OF BEING BLIND IS THAT I SOMETIMES LURK IN DARK PLACES AND HEAR THINGS NOT MEANT FOR MY EARS...
WE SHALL QUESTION HOLLY HERE AND NOW!

6/8
Copyright 1955, Field Enterprises, Inc.
Registered U. S. Patent Office.
MILTON CANIFF
MOTHER, NAMU SAID YOU WANTED TO SEE ME--OH, HELLO, STEVE!
HELLO, HOLLY
HOLLY, LAMB, WERE YOU OUT OF THIS HOUSE TONIGHT?
YOU SEEM TO HESITATE, HONEY! I KNOW RIGHT WELL THAT YOU WOULDN'T LIE TO ME, SO IS THERE SOME OTHER REASON THAT YOU DELAY ANSWERING?
YES, MOTHER, I WAS OUT...
YOU MUST HAVE HAD A MIGHTY GOOD REASON FOR DISOBEYING YOUR FATHER'S DIRECT ORDER THAT YOU WERE NOT TO GO OUT ALONE AT NIGHT!
REED IS BEING SHIPPED OUT- I HAD TO SEE HIM! I-I LOVE HIM, MOTHER!
VERY WELL! WE'LL DISCUSS THAT LATER, DEAR... NOW, STEVE, PLEASE TELL US THE BAD NEWS THAT CAUSED YOU TO SCURRY OVER HERE TO PROTECT US!

6/9
Copyright 1955, Field Enterprises, Inc.
MILTON CANIFF
REED KIMBERLY WENT A.W.O.L. TO SAY GOODBYE TO HOLLY BEFORE HIS OUTFIT MOVED OUT...THEY WERE TO MEET AT THE BLUE CAT CAFE IN THE OLD CITY...
THE PLACE WAS RAIDED AND A VIAL OF BLACK MARKET POLIO VACCINE WAS FOUND IN THE CROWN OF REED'S CAP...
THE SHORE PATROL SAW A BLONDE GIRL TO WHOM REED CALLED 'RUN'! SHE GOT AWAY, BUT THEY FOUND HOLLY'S IDENTITY CARD IN THE DARK HALLWAY
SINCE REED WAS PART OF THE GUARD AT THE NAVY HOSPITAL, WHERE VACCINE IS STORED, THE CIRCUMSTANTIAL EVIDENCE IS HEAVY AGAINST HIM...
IF REED IS COURT-MARTIALED, HOLLY'S NAME WILL SURELY COME INTO THE TRIAL... TELL ME, HOLLY, HONEY, DID YOU AND REED HAVE ANYTHING TO DO WITH THE VACCINE...
OH, MOTHER, NO! HOW IN THE WORLD COULD YOU EVEN TH---
HUSH, LAMB! -I MERELY WANTED TO HEAR YOU DENY IT! NOW GO TO YOUR ROOM!

6/10
MILTON CANIFF
Copyright 1955, Field Enterprises, Inc. Registered U.S. Patent Office.
WOULD YOU LIKE ME TO GO, GIL?
NO, STEVE, I-I RECKON I HAD TO CATCH MY WIND AND MY WITS... I AM DEEPLY GRATEFUL THAT YOU ARE HERE... ESPECIALLY WITH HOMER AWAY...
I MUST PREPARE TO DEFEND MY LITTLE GIRL —AND I'D BE OBLIGED IF YOU WOULD ALLOW ME TO TAKE COURAGE FROM YOUR STRENGTH
I'M HONORED, GIL, BUT DO YOU THINK YOU'RE UP TO THE PHYSICAL EFFORT THIS MAY REQUIRE?
YOU MEAN—WHAT CAN A BLIND WOMAN DO TO SAVE HER CHILD FROM DISGRACE? —I DON'T KNOW... BUT IF YOU WILL FIND ME THE MOUNTAIN, I SHALL MOVE IT!

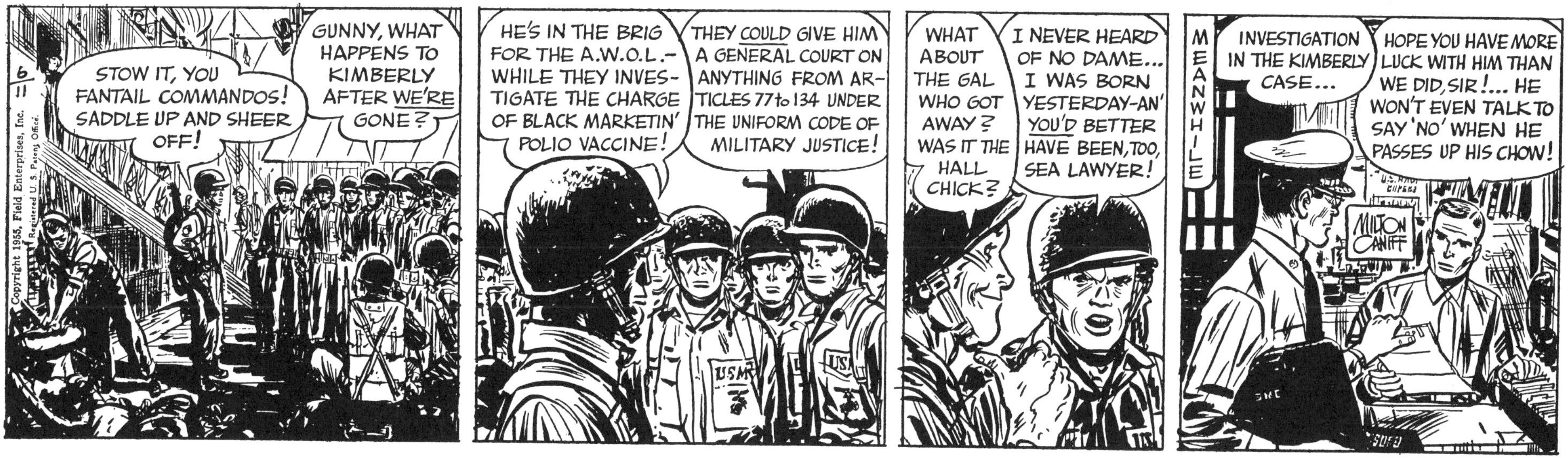
6/11
Copyright 1955, Field Enterprises, Inc. Registered U.S. Patent Office.
STOW IT, YOU FANTAIL COMMANDOS! SADDLE UP AND SHEER OFF!
GUNNY, WHAT HAPPENS TO KIMBERLY AFTER WE'RE GONE?
HE'S IN THE BRIG FOR THE A.W.O.L.— WHILE THEY INVESTIGATE THE CHARGE OF BLACK MARKETIN' POLIO VACCINE!
THEY COULD GIVE HIM A GENERAL COURT ON ANYTHING FROM ARTICLES 77 to 134 UNDER THE UNIFORM CODE OF MILITARY JUSTICE!
WHAT ABOUT THE GAL WHO GOT AWAY? WAS IT THE HALL CHICK?
I NEVER HEARD OF NO DAME... I WAS BORN YESTERDAY-AN' YOU'D BETTER HAVE BEEN, TOO, SEA LAWYER!
MEANWHILE
INVESTIGATION IN THE KIMBERLY CASE...
HOPE YOU HAVE MORE LUCK WITH HIM THAN WE DID, SIR!... HE WON'T EVEN TALK TO SAY 'NO' WHEN HE PASSES UP HIS CHOW!
MILTON CANIFF

STEVE CANYON®
by MILTON CANIFF
STEVE, THE POLICE BELIEVE THAT REED KIMBERLY AND MY DAUGHTER HOLLY WERE INVOLVED IN A BLACK MARKET OPERATION IN POLIO VACCINE...
HOLLY DENIES IT, AND THAT IS ALL THE EVIDENCE I NEED... BUT THE WORLD IS NOT HER MOTHER, SO IT DEMANDS MORE TANGIBLE PROOF...
THIS I INTEND TO SUPPLY, WITHOUT DISTRACTING HER FATHER FROM HIS DELICATE DIPLOMATIC MISSION IN JAPAN...
...I HOPE YOU ARE WITH ME, STEVE CANYON, BUT WHETHER YOU ARE OR NOT, I AM GOING FORWARD WITH IT...

THERE!—I HAVE MADE MY NOBLE SPEECH—YOU MAY LAUGH AT ME NOW...
I'M NOT LAUGHING, GIL... I AM JUST GLAD I'M ON YOUR SIDE!
SINCE THE SERUM SOMEONE PLANTED IN REED KIMBERLY'S MARINE CAP MUST HAVE BEEN FLOWN HERE, THE AIR FORCE HAS PUT ME ON THIS JOB...
OH, STEVE, I'M SO HAPPY I COULD BLUBBER...
I TALK BIG AND FINE, BUT I'M DOWNRIGHT SCARED SILLY, AND YOU KNOW IT! WHAT IN THE WIDE WORLD CAN A BLIND WOMAN DO TO HELP THOSE CHILDREN?
MORE THAN YOU MIGHT THINK—ALTHOUGH I WOULD NEVER HAVE ASKED YOU!

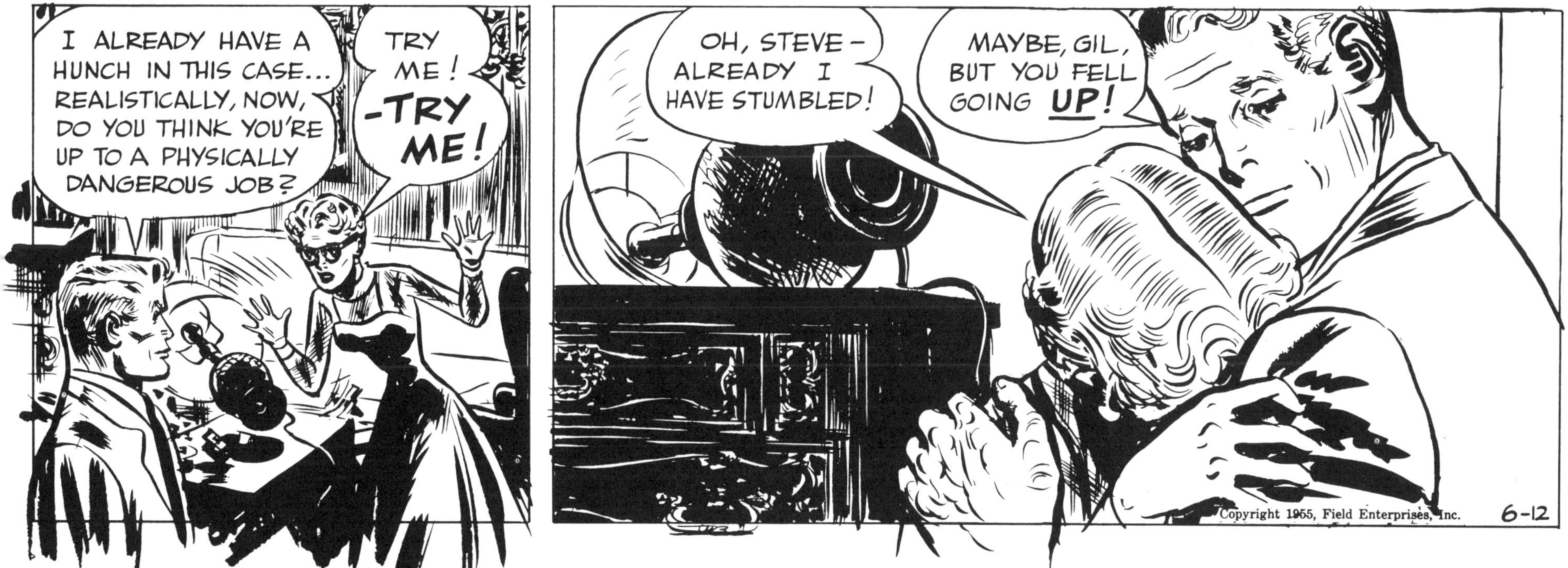
I ALREADY HAVE A HUNCH IN THIS CASE... REALISTICALLY, NOW, DO YOU THINK YOU'RE UP TO A PHYSICALLY DANGEROUS JOB?
TRY ME! -TRY ME!
OH, STEVE—ALREADY I HAVE STUMBLED!
MAYBE, GIL, BUT YOU FELL GOING UP!
Copyright 1955, Field Enterprises, Inc.
6-12

6/13
Copyright 1955, Field Enterprises, Inc. Registered U. S. Patent Office.
STEVE, I HOPE IT DOESN'T SOUND LIKE MOCK HEROICS...
..BUT I AM READY TO DO ANYTHING YOU SAY TO KEEP HOLLY FROM BEING SUSPECTED OF BLACK-MARKETEERING IN POLIO VACCINE!
I'LL TRY TO DO A FANCY STALLING JOB ON THE INVESTIGATION OF WHY REED HAD THE VACCINE IN HIS CAP...
LATER
WHO ARE YOU KIDDING, CANYON? WE ALL KNOW IT WAS PROBABLY THE HALL GIRL KIMBERLY WAS MEETING IN THAT NATIVE JOINT!
MAYBE, BUT UNTIL HE SAYS SO ON THE RECORD SHE IS NOT INVOLVED! —RIGHT?
MILTON CANIFF
SO HE CLAMS UP, WHILE YOU DO YOUR SLEUTHING TO CLEAR HIM AND KEEP THE GIRL'S NAME OUT OF IT, HUH?... I WISH YOU WERE BACK HOME LOOKING AFTER MY KIDS!

6/14
Copyright 1955, Field Enterprises, Inc. Registered U. S. Patent Office.
HONORABLE INN KEEPER, THE YELLOW HAIR IS OF THE AMERICAN MILITARY INTELLIGENCE...
...IT IS HIS WHIM TO PROD AMONG THE SWEEPINGS OF THIS HOSTELRY FOR BITS OF EVIDENCE...YOU KNOW—LIKE IN THE MOVIES!
HE HAS BEEN HOURS AT THIS TASK! WHAT DOES HE HOPE TO DISCOVER? THIS INN IS 100 YEARS OLD
BEHOLD! HE RISES FROM HIS GRUBBING! THE PRIZE IS BUT A SHRED OF PAPER!
MILTON CANIFF
LIEUTENANT, THIS IS CANYON! I FOUND A CHEWING-GUM WRAPPER FROM GREAT CIRCLE AIRLINES AT THE BLUE CAT CAFE!...
GET ME A LIST OF THE MOST RECENT G.C.A. ARRIVALS FROM THE UNITED STATES!
DARN CLEVER, THESE AMERICANS!

6/15
Copyright 1955, Field Enterprises, Inc.
Registered U.S. Patent Office.
THERE WERE MANY OCCIDENTALS IN THE BLUE CAT CAFE THE NIGHT KIMBERLY IS ALLEGED TO HAVE HAD BLACK-MARKET POLIO VACCINE HIDDEN IN HIS CAP...
IN THE CAFE DEBRIS I FOUND THIS GREAT CIRCLE AIRLINES CHEWING-GUM WRAPPER! SOME LINES GIVE YOU GUM JUST BEFORE LANDING...
MOST PEOPLE WOULD CHEW EVEN A SPARE PIECE WITHIN HOURS AFTER ARRIVAL...
LIST OF RECENT AIRLINE ARRIVALS, SIR...
NONE OF THEM TAGGED FOR POLICE OBSERVATION! — SEE ANY NAMES YOU RECOGNIZE?
YES — I SEE ONE, BUT MAYBE I KNOW JUST ENOUGH ABOUT IT TO GET US INTO TROUBLE!
MILTON CANIFF

6/16
Copyright 1955, Field Enterprises, Inc.
Registered U.S. Patent Office.
DID YOU GET ME A CREDIT CHECK ON THE MAN WHOSE NAME WAS ON THE AIRLINE PASSENGER LIST?
YES... STATESIDE SAYS YOUR BOY HAS HAD SOME BAD BREAKS LATELY, WENT BANKRUPT, BUT NO POLICE RECORD...
MILTON CANIFF
LOCAL POLICE SAY THE MAN IS NOW REGISTERED AT THIS HOTEL...CUSTOMS ENTRY DECLARATION STATES HE IS ON PERSONAL BUSINESS...
THANKS
YESSOR, I TAKE CHIT TO---
HOLD IT! HERE HE COMES NOW---
ROY HIMMERSKORN!

6 17
Copyright 1955, Field Enterprises, Inc.
Registered U. S. Patent Office.
ROY HIMMERSKORN! I DIDN'T EXPECT TO SEE YOU IN FORMOSA! HOW ARE YOU?
WHY-AH-FINE, CANYON... HAVEN'T SEEN YOU SINCE OUR LITTLE CANADIAN JUNKET... WHAT'S YOUR LINE NOW?
I'M STILL IN THE AIR FORCE-ON A LIAISON JOB WITH THE U.S. CONSULATE
I MUST ARRANGE TO MEET THE PEOPLE AT THE CONSULATE! ...I'M HERE TO INVEST IN LOCAL INDUSTRY...
I'M DUE OUT THERE FOR TEA SOON...WHY DON'T I SET UP AN INVITATION FOR YOU?
HEY! YOU TURNED OUT TO BE A PAL!
MEANWHILE...
KIMBERLY, HOW LONG DO YOU THINK YOU CAN HOLD UP THIS INVESTIGATION BY NOT TALKING?
SIR, I DON'T KNOW!..I DON'T KNOW ANYTHING, SIR! EXCEPT THAT I'M MISERABLE!
MILTON CANIFF

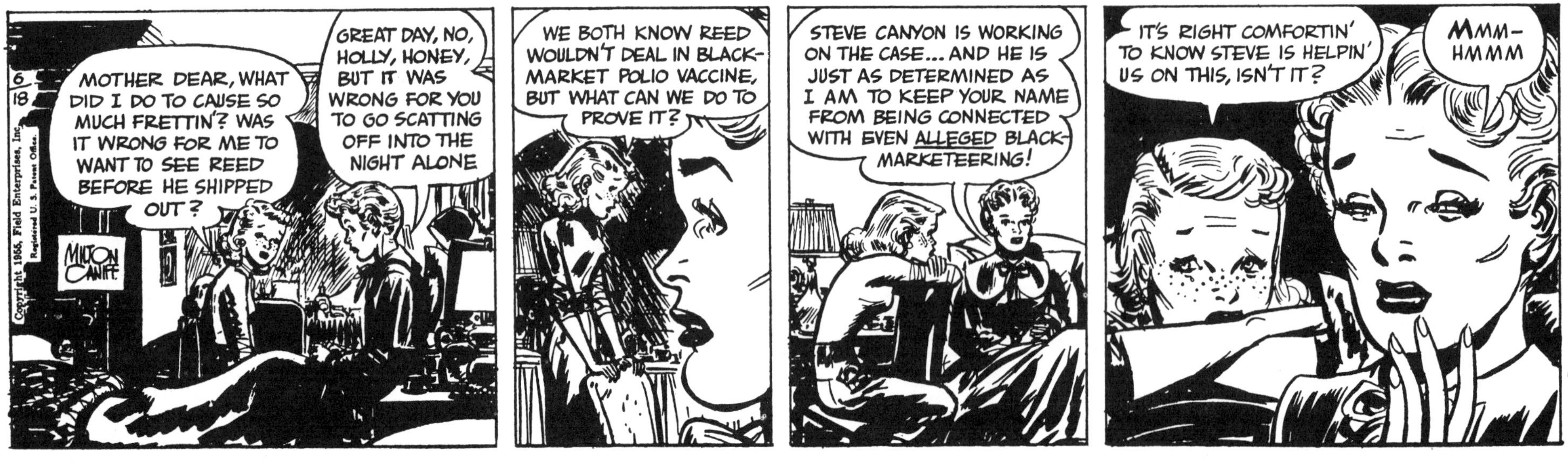
6 18
Copyright 1955, Field Enterprises, Inc.
Registered U. S. Patent Office.
MOTHER DEAR, WHAT DID I DO TO CAUSE SO MUCH FRETTIN'? WAS IT WRONG FOR ME TO WANT TO SEE REED BEFORE HE SHIPPED OUT?
GREAT DAY, NO, HOLLY, HONEY, BUT IT WAS WRONG FOR YOU TO GO SCATTING OFF INTO THE NIGHT ALONE
MILTON CANIFF
WE BOTH KNOW REED WOULDN'T DEAL IN BLACK-MARKET POLIO VACCINE, BUT WHAT CAN WE DO TO PROVE IT?
STEVE CANYON IS WORKING ON THE CASE... AND HE IS JUST AS DETERMINED AS I AM TO KEEP YOUR NAME FROM BEING CONNECTED WITH EVEN ALLEGED BLACK-MARKETEERING!
IT'S RIGHT COMFORTIN' TO KNOW STEVE IS HELPIN' US ON THIS, ISN'T IT?
MMM-HMMM

STEVE CANYON
MILTON CANIFF
GIL, ARE YOU SURE YOU STILL WANT TO GO THROUGH WITH THIS ?
STEVE, IF REED KIMBERLY IS COURT-MARTIALED FOR BLACK MARKETEERING, I RECKON HOLLY'S NAME WILL COME INTO IT! I DON'T INTEND TO HAVE THAT HAPPEN!
OKAY, THEN! BY PUTTING SEVERAL ITEMS TOGETHER WE HAVE CONCLUDED THAT A MAN NAMED ROY HIMMERSKORN WAS IN THE RESTAURANT BOOTH NEXT TO REED KIMBERLY AND COULD HAVE SLIPPED THE VIAL OF SERUM INTO THE BOY'S CAP AS IT HUNG ON THE RACK...
I'VE HEARD OF THIS HIMMERSKORN! DIDN'T HE JUST NOW COME TO FORMOSA ?
YES — AND MY THEORY MAY BE ALL WET — BUT HERE'S WHAT I WANT YOU TO DO...
MEANWHILE...
LOOK, KIMBERLY, I'M YOUR LAWYER! HOW CAN I DEFEND YOU IF YOU WON'T TALK ?
I'M SORRY, SIR — I-I JUST CAN'T!

AND IN A HOTEL IN THE CITY...
GENTLEMEN, YOU MAY TELL YOUR COMPANIES THAT HIMMERSKORN IS PREPARED TO INVEST IN THE FUTURE OF YOUR COUNTRY!
AND NOW, IF YOU WILL EXCUSE ME, I HAVE A VERY IMPORTANT ENGAGEMENT!
WELL, CANYON - MIGHTY NICE OF YOU TO GET ME AN INVITATION TO THE U.S. CONSULATE
AFTER THAT LITTLE MISADVENTURE WE HAD IN CANADA A COUPLE OF YEARS AGO I WASN'T SURE HOW I STOOD WITH YOU...
WE WERE ALL UNDER STRESS THEN, MR. HIMMERSKORN... SORRY MR. HALL IS AWAY, BUT HIS WIFE IS A GRACIOUS HOSTESS...
YOU'LL FIND IT HARD TO REALIZE THAT SHE IS TOTALLY BLIND!
IS THAT SO? WELL, WELL!
GIL, I WANT YOU TO KNOW MR. ROY HIMMERSKORN. HE'S OUT HERE ON BUSINESS!
H-HOW DO YOU DO, MRS. HALL!
WELL, MIS-TER HIMMERSKORN! I'VE HEARD SO MUCH ABOUT YOU! I DECLARE IT'S A GENUINE PLEASURE TO MEET YOU! YOU COME SIT RIGHT HERE BESIDE ME AND TELL ME WHAT ALL IS HAPPENING IN YOUR BUSY LIFE!
WHY-AH-YES, I WILL-THANK YOU...
Copyright 1955, Field Enterprises, Inc.
6-19

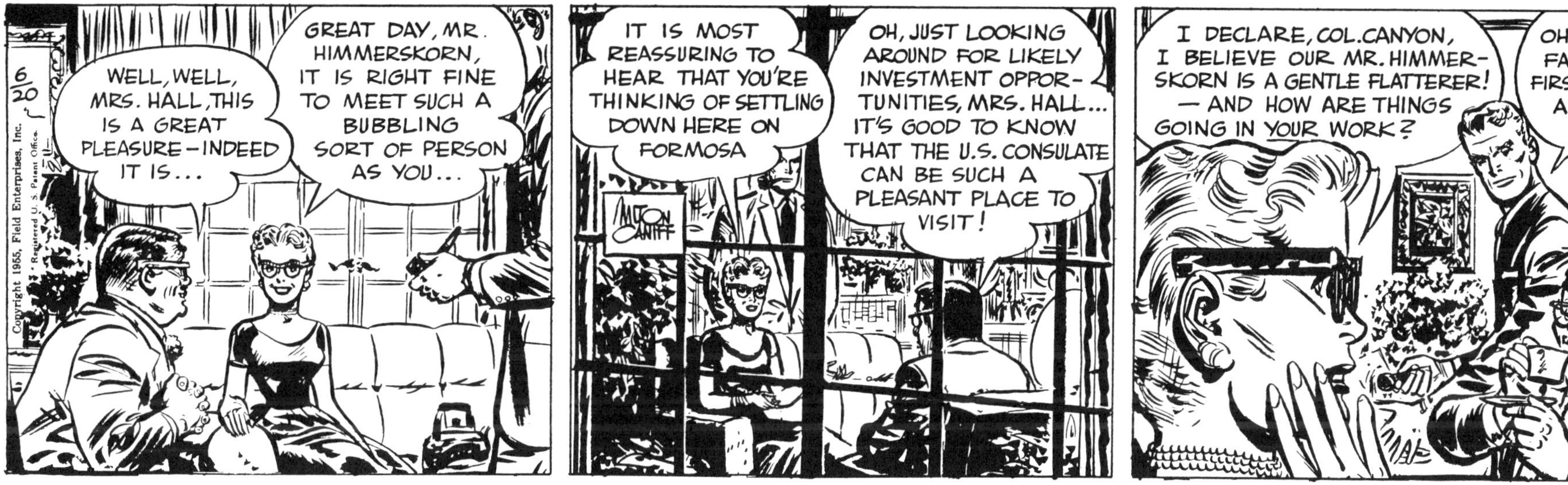
6/20
Copyright 1955, Field Enterprises, Inc.
WELL, WELL, MRS. HALL, THIS IS A GREAT PLEASURE—INDEED IT IS...
GREAT DAY, MR. HIMMERSKORN, IT IS RIGHT FINE TO MEET SUCH A BUBBLING SORT OF PERSON AS YOU...
IT IS MOST REASSURING TO HEAR THAT YOU'RE THINKING OF SETTLING DOWN HERE ON FORMOSA
OH, JUST LOOKING AROUND FOR LIKELY INVESTMENT OPPORTUNITIES, MRS. HALL... IT'S GOOD TO KNOW THAT THE U.S. CONSULATE CAN BE SUCH A PLEASANT PLACE TO VISIT!
MILTON CANIFF
I DECLARE, COL. CANYON, I BELIEVE OUR MR. HIMMERSKORN IS A GENTLE FLATTERER! —AND HOW ARE THINGS GOING IN YOUR WORK?
OH, FINE SO FAR, GIL... FIRST CLASS ALL THE WAY!

6/21
Copyright 1955, Field Enterprises, Inc.
GREAT DAY IN THE MORNING, MR. HIMMERSKORN... I DO WISH MR. HALL WERE BACK FROM JAPAN... HE WOULD LOVE YOUR STORIES—
CANYON, I DIDN'T EXPECT TO BE MADE SO WELCOME OUT HERE... I CAN THANK YOU FOR IT.
I SUPPOSE WE 'FOREIGNERS' ARE DRAWN TOGETHER IN THESE FAR PLACES —SHARING COMMON DANGERS AND SO ON...
DO YOU THINK THERE WILL BE A WAR?
ASIDE FROM THAT... MRS. HALL WORRIES ABOUT HER LOVELY YOUNG DAUGHTER COMING DOWN WITH A RARE DISEASE THIS FAR FROM THE STATES.
THE GIRL MIGHT EVEN CONTRACT POLIO —AND SHE ISN'T ELIGIBLE FOR SHOTS OF THAT NEW VACCINE!
MILTON CANIFF

6/22
Copyright 1955, Field Enterprises, Inc. Registered U.S. Patent Office.
MRS. HALL, WHAT DO YOU MEAN YOUR LOVELY DAUGHTER ISN'T ELIGIBLE FOR POLIO VACCINE SHOTS?
SHE ISN'T A CHILD, MR. HIMMERSKORN —BUT SHE COULD CATCH POLIO AS EASILY AS IF SHE WERE...
THE NAVY HOSPITAL HAS THE VACCINE FOR SERVICE CHILDREN, BUT WE CIVILIANS CANNOT IN CONSCIENCE ASK THEM FOR IT...
BUT LOOK HERE, GENTLEMEN, I DIDN'T RIGHTLY INTEND TO BURDEN YOU WITH MY TROUBLES... WILL YOU HAVE MORE TEA...?
NO BURDEN AT ALL, MRS. HALL... YOU SOUNDED DESPERATE ABOUT THE VACCINE...
I AM... I WOULD GIVE ANYTHING I OWN TO KNOW HOLLY WAS IMMUNE TO POLIO...
MILTON CANIFF
HMM...

6/23
Copyright 1955, Field Enterprises, Inc. Registered U.S. Patent Office.
WELL, HIMMERSKORN, WHAT DO YOU THINK OF MRS. HALL?
FASCINATING! —SO PRETTY AND YET— SHE'S BLIND!
SHE HAS TRAINED HERSELF WELL, BUT THE FEAR OF HER DAUGHTER CATCHING POLIO HAS HER SHOWING THE STRAIN!
BUT SHE'S A DIPLOMAT'S WIFE... WHY COULDN'T SHE FINAGLE SOME SHOTS FROM THE NAVY?
SHE'D GIVE HER LIFE FOR THE GIRL, BUT SHE WOULDN'T THINK OF ASKING FOR SPECIAL PRIVILEGES!
SHE WOULDN'T HAVE TO ASK ME!
MILTON CANIFF
UNFORTUNATELY YOU'RE NOT IN A POSITION TO GRANT WHAT SHE WANTS!
THAT'S WHAT YOU TH--- I MEAN —YES, OF COURSE... I'M IN NO POSITION!

6/24
Copyright 1955, Field Enterprises, Inc. Registered U. S. Patent Office.
THAT MRS. HALL... BEAUTIFUL WOMAN ...CAN'T SEE A THING! WHAD'YA KNOW!
HOW CAN SHE BE SO SMARTLY TURNED OUT WHEN SHE CAN'T EVEN SEE TO PUT ON LIPSTICK?
SHE'S DESPERATE TO GET POLIO VACCINE SHOTS FOR HER DAUGHTER! HUSBAND'S OUT OF TOWN...WELL, WELL!
STEADY, HIMMERSKORN! –GOTTA STICK STRICTLY TO BUSINESS OUT HERE! ...SKIN JUST LIKE MARBLE...
MILTON CANIFF
TAKE ME TO THE U.S. CONSULATE!

6/25
Copyright 1955, Field Enterprises, Inc. Registered U. S. Patent Office.
KIMBERLY, YOU'RE GETTING BREAKS YOU PROBABLY DON'T DESERVE!
WE KNOW THAT POLIO VACCINE FOUND IN YOUR CAP WAS INTENDED FOR THE BLACK MARKET AND PROBABLY FOR THE COMMIES, BUT WHO CAN PROVE IT?
...WE KNOW IT WAS PROBABLY THE HALL GIRL WHO CAME TO MEET YOU...
BUT CAN SHE AS A U.S. CIVILIAN CITIZEN BE FORCED TO TESTIFY AT A MILITARY COURT WHEN WE'RE NOT IN U.S. TERRITORY?
MEANWHILE... AT THE U.S. CONSULATE
YOU REMEMBER ME, DON'T YOU? I AM ROY HIMMERSKORN...I'D LIKE TO SEE MRS. HALL...IT'S–AH–WELL, AN EMERGENCY
PLEASED TO WAIT, SOR. I GO SEE...
MILTON CANIFF

STEVE CANYON
by MILTON CANIFF
WHY ALL THE BOOKS, RUSS? YOU LOOK LIKE EXAM TIME AT THE ACADEMY!
I'M DEFENDING THAT MARINE NAMED KIMBERLY IN THE POLIO VACCINE BLACK MARKET CASE, AND HE WON'T TALK—EVEN TO ME!
MOTHER DEAR, CAN'T I EVEN GO SEE REED KIMBERLY? I FEEL LIKE A DESERTER!
COMPOSE YOURSELF, HOLLY, LAMB!... STEVE CANYON IS WORKING ON REED'S CASE AND HE SAYS FOR YOU TO STAY AWAY!
LATER
MIZZUS HALL, IS MIZT ROY HIMMERSKORN ASK COULD COME SEE!
WHY, YES, NAMU! IT MUST BE AN EMERGENCY!
MIZT HIMMER-SKORN
MR. HIMMERSKORN, I DO HOPE YOU'LL FORGIVE MY TACKY APPEARANCE! MY DAUGHTER DRESSES ME—AND SHE HAS GONE TO BED
WHY—AH—OF COURSE! I DIDN'T THINK OF THAT!

I AM COMPLETELY A CREATURE OF MY CHILD'S GOOD TASTE... SHE BUYS ALL MY CLOTHING, DOES MY HAIR AND MAKEUP
SHE MUST BE A REMARKABLE YOUNG WOMAN!
YES, SHE IS! I WOULD DO ANYTHING FOR HER, BUT WITH MY HANDICAP SHE MIGHT VERY WELL CATCH AN ASIATIC ILLNESS BECAUSE I COULDN'T RECOGNIZE THE SYMPTOMS!
DOESN'T HER FATHER TAKE CARE OF SUCH MATTERS?
HE DOES HIS BEST BUT, FOR INSTANCE, HE IS AWAY RIGHT NOW AND THERE ARE NO MEANS FOR ME TO TRY AND ARRANGE FOR HER TO HAVE POLIO VACCINE SHOTS...
THE NAVAL HOSPITAL HAS THE SERUM FOR THE CHILDREN OF MILITARY PERSONNEL, BUT WE ARE NOT MILITARY, AND HOLLY IS NOT A CHILD... SO YOU CAN UNDERSTAND MY CONCERN...
OF COURSE, MRS. HALL
... BUT YOU DID NOT COME HERE TO LISTEN TO MY TROUBLES, MR. HIMMER-SKORN! I DO DECLARE, I DIDN'T ASK WHAT IT WAS YOU WANTED TO SEE ME ABOUT...
OH–THAT CAN WAIT... I AM MOST IMPRESSED BY HOW DEEPLY YOU LOVE YOUR DAUGHTER—AND THAT YOU DESPERATELY WISH HER TO HAVE THE POLIO VACCINE! —JUST HOW DESPERATELY, MRS. HALL?
Copyright 1955, Field Enterprises, Inc.
6-26

6/27
Copyright 1955, Field Enterprises, Inc. Registered U. S. Patent Office
MRS. HALL, I CAME BACK WITHOUT CANYON TO TELL YOU I MIGHT BE ABLE TO ARRANGE FOR YOUR DAUGHTER TO GET POLIO VACCINE INJECTIONS!
W-WHY, MR. HIMMERSKORN! HOW IN THE WIDE WORLD COULD YOU---
NO ONE MUST HEAR OF THIS...NOT YOUR HUSBAND, OR STEVE CANYON, OR EVEN THE GIRL! SHE CAN THINK IT IS A VITAMIN SHOT—OR SOME SUCH...
BUT I HAVE VERY LITTLE MONEY! HOW COULD I PAY?
I AM SO IMPRESSED BY YOUR DEVOTION TO YOUR DAUGHTER THAT MONEY IS NOT OF FIRST IMPORTANCE —AS LONG AS YOU DO WHAT I SAY...
I AM LISTENING— VERY CAREFULLY!
MILTON CANIFF

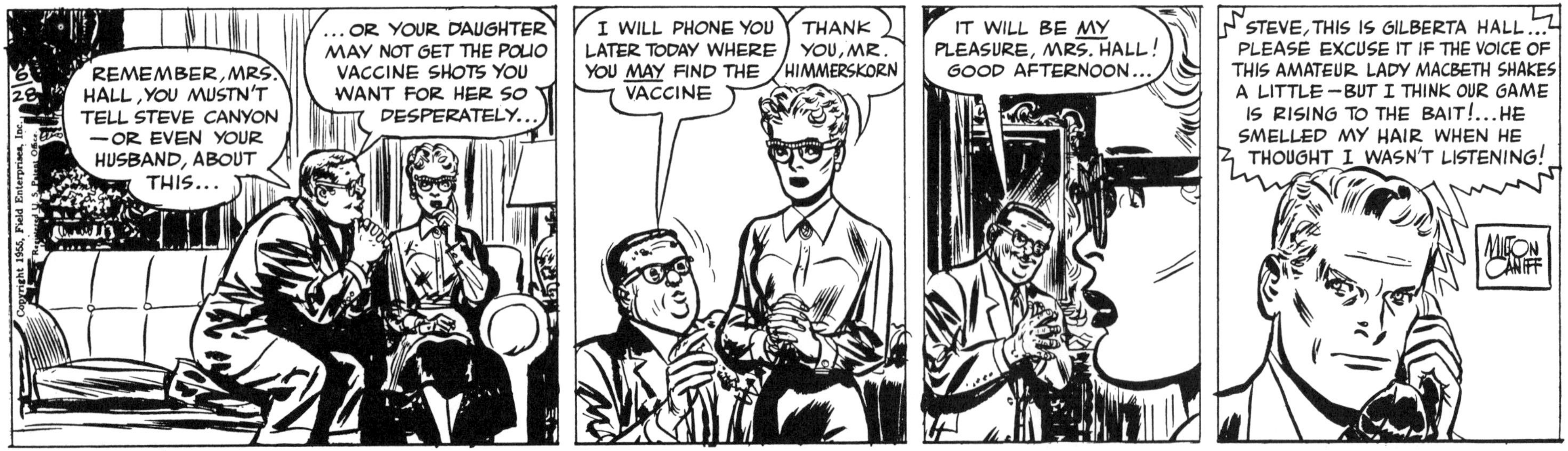
6/28
Copyright 1955, Field Enterprises, Inc. Registered U. S. Patent Office
REMEMBER, MRS. HALL, YOU MUSTN'T TELL STEVE CANYON —OR EVEN YOUR HUSBAND, ABOUT THIS...
...OR YOUR DAUGHTER MAY NOT GET THE POLIO VACCINE SHOTS YOU WANT FOR HER SO DESPERATELY...
I WILL PHONE YOU LATER TODAY WHERE YOU MAY FIND THE VACCINE
THANK YOU, MR. HIMMERSKORN
IT WILL BE MY PLEASURE, MRS. HALL! GOOD AFTERNOON...
STEVE, THIS IS GILBERTA HALL... PLEASE EXCUSE IT IF THE VOICE OF THIS AMATEUR LADY MACBETH SHAKES A LITTLE—BUT I THINK OUR GAME IS RISING TO THE BAIT!...HE SMELLED MY HAIR WHEN HE THOUGHT I WASN'T LISTENING!
MILTON CANIFF

6/29
..SO THAT'S WHAT HAPPENED, STEVE! NOW I AM TO WAIT FOR A CALL FROM HIMMERSKORN...THEN I WILL GO TO A PLACE HE NAMES TO GET THE POLIO VACCINE FOR HOLLY...
HE'S SHREWD, GIL...AND WE STILL HAVE NO EVIDENCE AGAINST HIM! I BROUGHT A PORTABLE WIRE RECORDER...
CARRY IT IN YOUR PURSE AND GET HIS ENTIRE PITCH FOR THE RECORD! I'LL SHOW YOU HOW TO WORK IT IN A MOMENT...
PHONE ME WHEN HE TELLS YOU THE ADDRESS, AND WE'LL GO RIGHT THERE TO STAND BY IF THE GOING GETS TOO ROUGH! BLOW THIS WHISTLE IF YOU NEED US!...
GIL, DO YOU STILL THINK YOU CAN HANDLE THIS? IT MIGHT BECOME REALLY DANGEROUS...
STEVE, YOU NEVER HAD A DAUGHTER WHO MIGHT BE DISGRACED BY BEING SUSPECTED OF A CRIME! ...I ONLY HOPE I MAY ACT AS WELL AS I CAN YEARN!
MILTON CANIFF

6/30
I DECLARE, MOTHER, DEAR, YOU DO LOOK AS PRETTY AS A QUEEN—IF I DO SAY SO MY VERY OWN SELF...
YOU'RE A LAMB TO WORK SO HARD ON MY APPEARANCE, HOLLY, HONEY! I ALWAYS HAVE SUCH CONFIDENCE WHEN YOU DRESS ME AND PUT ON MY MAKEUP!
I'M GOIN' STARK, STARIN' CRAZY WITH REED KIMBERLY SITTIN' IN THAT OL' BRIG! I'M HAPPY WE'RE SETTIN' OUT ON YOUR CHARITY CALLS...
WHY, AH - I WON'T BE MAKING THE USUAL ROUNDS...I'LL GO DOWNTOWN ALONE
BUT, MOTHER, YOU CAN'T GO OUT WITHOUT A COMPANION...
MILTON CANIFF
- I KNOW...
I'M TAKING A TAXICAB - AND MEETING SOMEONE IN THE CITY WHO WILL ESCORT ME...

7/1
Copyright 1955, Field Enterprises, Inc.
Registered U.S. Patent Office.
HOLLY, HONEY, I DECLARE I DIDN'T MEAN TO HURT YOUR FEELINGS!
ORDINARILY I WOULD WANT YOU TO TAKE ME DOWN-TOWN, BUT THIS IS A—WELL, A SORT OF SECURITY MISSION FOR THE GOVERNMENT...
HOLLY, BABY! PLEASE—DON'T BE H--
MIZ HALL—IS MAN ON TELEPHONE—NO SAY WHO NAME!
MRS. HALL, YOU KNOW WHO THIS IS...THE ADDRESS IS NUMBER 19 STREET OF THE WATER BIRDS! A TAXICAB SHOULD BE WAITING OUTSIDE THE CONSULATE FOR YOU AT THIS MOMENT!
I'M SORRY, MA'AM. COLONEL CANYON WAS JUST CALLED INTO THE ADMIRAL'S OFFICE FOR A CONFERENCE ON THE CASE HE IS ASSIGNED TO...
OH, DEAR... WELL, WILL YOU TELL HIM THAT GIL CALLED?.. THE ADDRESS HE WANTED IS NO. 19 STREET OF THE WATER BIRDS—I HAVE TO RUN NOW...
MILTON CANIFF

7/2
Copyright 1955, Field Enterprises, Inc.
NAMU, DON'T LET HOLLY OUT OF YOUR SIGHT... I'LL BE BACK JUST AS SOON AS EVER I CAN!
SO WILL DO, MIZ HALL!
MILTON CANIFF
DRIVER, YOU KNOW YOU ARE TO TAKE ME TO NO. 19 STREET OF THE WATER BIRDS?
AH, SO, MIZ...
... AND THEY DRIVE AWAY... BUT IT IS NOT NO. 19 STREET OF THE WATER BIRDS AT WHICH THE CAB STOPS...
THIS PLACE, MIZ...
GOOD...WILL YOU LEAD ME TO THE DOOR?
MEANWHILE...
THE ADMIRAL GAVE YOU MORE TIME ON THE KIMBERLY CASE, CANYON, BUT DON'T HOLD US UP UNTIL WORLD WAR THREE!
PHONE MESSAGE FOR YOU, COL. CANYON—THE LADY SAID SHE COULDN'T WAIT...

STEVE CANYON
by MILTON CANIFF
CANYON, WE CAN'T DELAY DISPOSITION OF THE KIMBERLY CASE MUCH LONGER! WHAT'S THE SCORE?
THERE WAS NO POLIO VACCINE MISSING FROM THE NAVY HOSPITAL! YOU'RE NOT GOING TO ASK FOR A GENERAL COURT FOR A FEW HOURS A.W.O.L., ARE YOU?
NO, BUT THERE WAS VACCINE MISSING BACK IN THE STATES — WHICH COULD HAVE BEEN FLOWN OUT TO THE MARINE!
THEN WHY WEREN'T HIS FINGER-PRINTS ON THE VIAL? PLEASE GIVE US A LITTLE MORE TIME!
NAVCOMSTA
MEANWHILE
NAMU, WHERE'S MY MOTHER? WHY DOESN'T ANYONE TELL ME ANYTHING?
MILLION PARDONS, MISSY HOLLY. NAMU GOT ORDERS TO KEEP EYE OPEN AT YOU — AN' MOUTH SHUT AT YOU!
AND IN A HOUSE IN THE OLD SECTION OF THE CITY
MR. HIMMERSKORN...
AH-H-H! MRS. HALL!

...AND NOW SHALL WE GET TO THE POINT? YOU SENT FOR ME, SO I ASSUME YOU HAVE POLIO VACCINE FOR MY DAUGHTER!
I SAID I MIGHT HAVE THE VACCINE
PLEASE DON'T TEASE ME, MR. HIMMERSKORN! I TOLD YOU I HAVEN'T MUCH MONEY!
IT ISN'T A MATTER OF MONEY... IT'S -IT'S...
... I AM FASCINATED BY YOU AND BY THIS SITUATION... AT THIS MOMENT YOU ARE COMPLETELY HELPLESS... YOU DON'T EVEN KNOW WHERE YOU ARE... AND YOU SEEK SOMETHING FROM ME...
I WANT YOU TO KISS ME!
WHAT ?
...IT WILL SOUND BAD ENOUGH THAT YOU TRIED TO GET BLACK MARKET POLIO SERUM FOR YOUR DAUGHTER, BUT EVEN WORSE THAT THE WIFE OF A CONSULAR OFFICIAL HELD A RENDEZVOUS WITH A MAN WHILE HER HUSBAND WAS AWAY...
YOU CAN BUY THE VACCINE AND MY SILENCE FOR A KISS!
Copyright 1955, Field Enterprises, Inc.
7-3

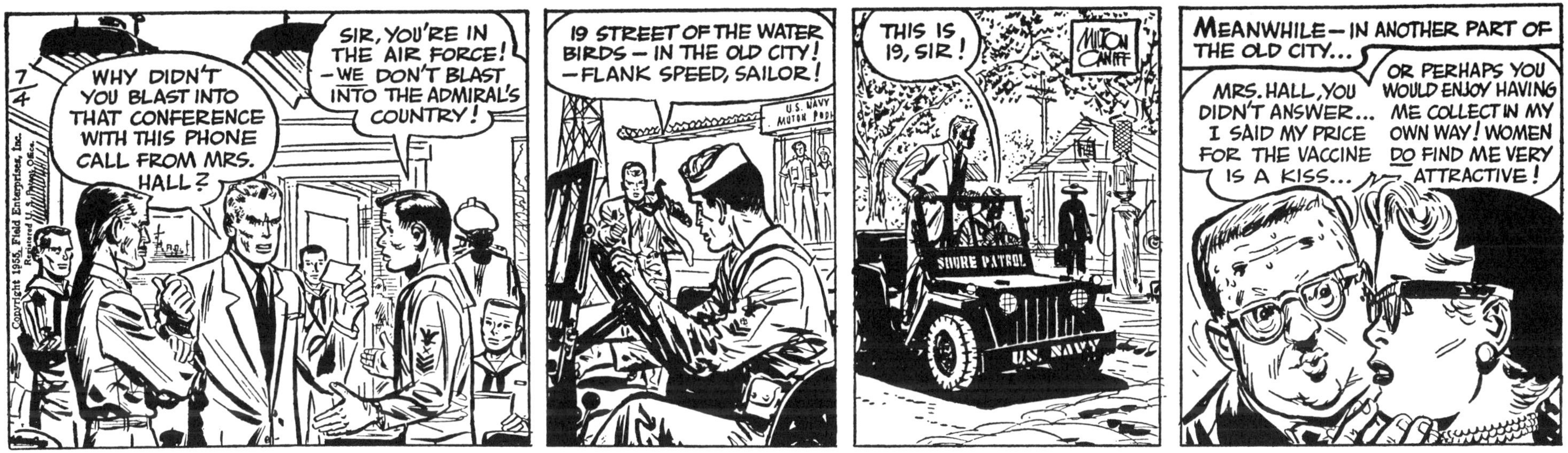
7/4
WHY DIDN'T YOU BLAST INTO THAT CONFERENCE WITH THIS PHONE CALL FROM MRS. HALL?
SIR, YOU'RE IN THE AIR FORCE! —WE DON'T BLAST INTO THE ADMIRAL'S COUNTRY!
Copyright 1955, Field Enterprises, Inc. Registered U.S. Patent Office.
19 STREET OF THE WATER BIRDS — IN THE OLD CITY! —FLANK SPEED, SAILOR!
U.S. NAVY
THIS IS 19, SIR!
MILTON CANIFF
SHORE PATROL
U.S. NAVY
MEANWHILE — IN ANOTHER PART OF THE OLD CITY...
MRS. HALL, YOU DIDN'T ANSWER... I SAID MY PRICE FOR THE VACCINE IS A KISS...
OR PERHAPS YOU WOULD ENJOY HAVING ME COLLECT IN MY OWN WAY! WOMEN DO FIND ME VERY ATTRACTIVE!

7/5
HIMMERSKORN MOUSETRAPPED ME — BUT GOOD! HE MUST HAVE SENT A STOOGE CABBY TO PICK UP MRS. HALL...
...WHO TOOK HER TO A DIFFERENT ADDRESS THAN THE ONE HE'D TOLD HER OVER THE PHONE!.. BEING BLIND, SHE WOULDN'T KNOW WHERE SHE WAS...
Copyright 1955, Field Enterprises, Inc. Registered U.S. Patent Office.
SHORE PATROL
U.S. NAVY
I KNEW I SHOULDN'T HAVE ALLOWED HER TO TALK ME INTO MAKING HER THE BAIT IN THIS DEAL — BUT IT'S TOO LATE TO KICK MYSELF NOW..
BOS'N, HERE'S WHAT WE DO...
MEANWHILE...
YOU'RE A SENSIBLE WOMAN... YOU'LL ENJOY KISSING ME... AND YOUR DAUGHTER WILL GET THE POLIO VACCINE...
THE WIRE RECORDER IN MY PURSE IS GOING... I MUST GET ALL THE EVIDENCE I CAN... AND I STILL HAVE THE WHISTLE! ...STEVE IS SURELY JUST OUTSIDE THE DOOR THIS MINUTE WAITING TO HEAR IT...
HOW CAN I BE GOOD AND CERTAIN I'LL GET THE POLIO VACCINE?
MILTON CANIFF

7/6
Copyright 1955, Field Enterprises, Inc. Registered U. S. Patent Office.
TO ALL SHORE PATROL JEEPS= PICK UP A ROY HIMMERSKORN, U.S. NATIONAL; CIVILIAN!..YOUR AUTHORITY ON THIS= LT. COL. S.B. CANYON, USAF.
WHO'S THAT JOKER ?
WHO EVER TELLS ME ANYTHING ? THE SCOOP IS THAT HE'S DAME CRAZY AND THEY PLANTED A GAL WITH A WIRE RECORDER TO NAIL HIM! —SOMETHING MUST HAVE FOULED UP!
MEANWHILE = IN THE OLD SECTION OF THE CITY...
HOW YOU JUST SIT THERE— COMPLETELY HELPLESS...
I'VE NEVER SEEN A WOMAN SO UTTERLY AT MY COMMAND
BUT I'M GOING TO COLLECT FOR THE POLIO VACCINE FOR YOUR DAUGHTER— SO LET ME PUT THAT PURSE ASIDE SO YOU MAY ENJOY KISSING ME!
NOW— I'LL HAVE TO BLOW THE WHISTLE NOW!
MILTON CANIFF

7/7
Copyright 1955, Field Enterprises, Inc. Registered U. S. Patent Office.
I'LL PUT YOUR PURSE OVER HERE, HONEY—SAY, WHAT HAVE YOU GOT IN THIS THING ? HEY!
—A WHISTLE!!
MILTON CANIFF
MEANWHILE — AT NAVY SHORE PATROL HEADQUARTERS...
COL. CANYON, ON YOUR CALL TO NAMU, THE SERVANT AT THE CONSULATE...HE SAYS THIS IS THE LICENSE NUMBER OF THE TAXICAB THAT PICKED UP MRS. HALL...

7/8
Copyright 1955, Field Enterprises, Inc. Registered U.S. Patent Office.
TRYING TO BLOW A WHISTLE...WHICH MEANS THAT YOU EXPECTED CANYON OR SOME OF HIS STOOGES TO BE STANDING BY!
WELL, HE WON'T BE, BABY, BECAUSE ROY HIMMERSKORN IS A CAREFUL MAN! I TOLD YOU TO COME TO NO.19 STREET OF THE WATER BIRDS, BUT THAT'S NOT WHERE THE TAXICAB DELIVERED YOU!
HEY!
I THOUGHT YOUR PURSE WAS MIGHTY HEAVY! THERE'S A WIRE RECORDER INSIDE! —WITH ALL MY TALK ABOUT GETTING POLIO VACCINE FOR YOU PRESERVED FOR POSTERITY!
YOU AND STEVE CANYON ALMOST BOXED ME IN—SO NOW I DON'T NEED TO BE CONSCIENCE-STRICKEN ABOUT ANYTHING.... KISSING YOU WILL JUST BE GOOD FUN!
MILTON CANIFF

7/9
Copyright 1955, Field Enterprises, Inc. Registered U.S. Patent Office.
NAMU! MY POOR DARLIN' MOTHER ISN'T IN HER ROOM—HER BED HASN'T BEEN SLEPT IN...
YOU'VE BEEN TELEPHONING PEOPLE AND DOIN' SECRET STUFF—NOW I WANT TO KNOW WHAT'S GOIN' ON!
OH, MIZZY HOLLY, SO SORRY—YOUR MAMA ORDER NAMU TO WATCH YOU BUT TO TELL YOU NOT SOMETHING!
ALL I KNOW IS THAT MY MOTHER ISN'T HERE—AND I'M GOING TO DO SOMETHING ABOUT IT!
MILTON CANIFF
MEANWHILE= AT THE NAVY SHORE PATROL STATION
WHO DID YOU SAY, MISS?
OH, PLEASE LISTEN, MISTER! I'M HOLLY HALL AT THE U.S. CONSULATE! AND MY BLIND MOTHER HAS BEEN MISSIN' ALL NIGHT LONG... HELP ME, PLEASE!

STEVE CANYON
by MILTON CANIFF
I SHOULD HAVE GUESSED THIS WAS A TRAP WHEN THAT CANYON WAS SO FRIENDLY TO ME!
LUCKY FOR ME THAT I SPOTTED THE WIRE RECORDER IN YOUR PURSE, MRS. HALL... I GO TO THE MOVIES TOO YOU KNOW!
YOU'RE HURTING ME!
THAT IS NOTHING COMPARED TO WHAT YOU AND CANYON WERE GOING TO DO TO ME!
BUT HIMMERSKORN IS NOT GOING TO PLAY BOOB FOR YOU TWO...
WHAT I'LL DO TO YOU WILL BE BLAMED ON THE CHINESE RED UNDERGROUND
AND NOBODY WILL KNOW THAT YOU EVER CAME TO MEET ME!

MEANWHILE
HEY CHARLIE! WE JUST GOT A CALL FROM A MISS HALL AT THE U.S. CONSULATE THAT HER BLIND MOTHER HAS BEEN MISSING ALL NIGHT...
OH NO! NO!
USM
PUT OUT A RADIO BULLETIN ON IT TO THE SHORE PATROL JEEPS!
PLEASE! I'M READY TO TALK!
ME RIGHT IN THE MIDDLE OF REPORTS AN' YOU DECIDE TO SOUND OFF...
ALL RIGHT, KIMBERLY, I'LL TELL THE LOO-TENINT YOU WANTA GIVE OUT...
F FIRE
ISHER
SIR, YOUR CLAM WANTS T'OPEN UP!
ABOUT TIME!... THE PAPERS ARE GETTING YELLOW
AS THE CELL DOOR OPENS, REED KIMBERLY CRASHES OUT...
7-10

7/11
Copyright 1955, Field Enterprises, Inc. Registered U.S. Patent Office.
SNAP OUT OF IT, HIMMERSKORN! —THINGS AREN'T GOING EXACTLY ACCORDING TO PLAN...
IT'S JUST A MATTER OF TIME BEFORE CANYON FINDS THE TAXI DRIVER WHO BROUGHT MRS. HALL OUT HERE
I'M IN THIS TOO FAR TO BACKTRACK NOW—AND THE BLIND WOMAN IS TOO FASCINATING FOR MERE BLACKMAIL!
I'LL NEVER GET AWAY WITH THE POLIO VACCINE DODGE NOW—SO I'M GOING TO USE MY ESCAPE HATCH—AND TAKE THIS LUSCIOUS THING WITH ME!
MILTON CANIFF
MEANWHILE
HEAR THIS, ALL STATIONS AND VEHICLES = BE ON ALERT FOR PRISONER ESCAPED FROM SHORE PATROL BRIG... NAME = P.F.C. REED KIMBERLY... DESCRIPTION IS AS FOLLOWS...
HEY! IT'S THAT GYRENE WHO GOT BOXED IN THE POLIO VACCINE BLACK MARKET!.. IF THEY CATCH HIM HE'LL WISH THEY HAD SHOT FIRST!
U.S. NAVY

7/12
Copyright 1955, Field Enterprises, Inc. Registered U.S. Patent Office.
FAT 'MERICAN PAY ME TO BRING BLIND WOMAN HERE TO NO. 25 STREET OF THE TALLOW MAKERS, NO MATTER WHERE SHE SAY TO GO!
ASK THE FORMOSA POLICE TO SEARCH THE PLACE
NOBODY THERE, COL. CANYON... BUT SIGNS OF A STRUGGLE—AND I FOUND THIS...
IT'S THE SMASHED-UP REMAINS OF MRS. HALL'S WIRE RECORDER!
MEANWHILE = AS THE SHORE PATROL NET GOES OUT FOR REED KIMBERLY, ESCAPED PRISONER...
ALL THE TALK I OVERHEARD FROM THE SHORE PATROL DISPATCHERS MAKES SENSE NOW...
NO ONE COULD TAKE A BLIND WOMAN OUT OF TOWN EXCEPT BY BOAT—SO THE WATERFRONT IS THE PLACE TO HELP HOLLY'S MOTHER!
MILTON CANIFF

7/13
Copyright 1955, Field Enterprises, Inc. Registered U.S. Patent Office.
WHOEVER WOULD TRY TO TAKE HOLLY'S MOTHER OUT OF THE CITY WOULDN'T RELY ON A SLOW JUNK...
ONLY ONE TRAMP FREIGHTER WITH STEAM UP TO GET UNDER WAY...
MILTON CANIFF
AND AS REED KIMBERLY QUIETLY CLIMBS ABOARD...
...STEVE CANYON ARRANGES BY CAR RADIO TO BLOCK EVERY EXIT FROM THE FORMOSAN CITY!
YOU SAY SOMETHING, SIR ?
JUST SORTA THINKING OUT LOUD!.. IF MR. HALL DOESN'T SHOOT ME FOR ALLOWING THIS TO HAPPEN —HE SHOULD!..

7/14
Copyright 1955, Field Enterprises, Inc. Registered U.S. Patent Office.
AS REED KIMBERLY CLIMBS THE LINES FROM THE DOCK TO THE "S.S. GONQUIN"
I'M IN THIS SO DEEP NOW I MIGHT AS WELL ENJOY IT, BABY!..I'M GOING TO THE BRIDGE TO SEE MY PAL THE SKIPPER!
MAY I HAVE THE KNITTING FROM MY BAG?..
WELL, SKIPPER, THE POLIO VACCINE BLACK MARKET DIDN'T WORK OUT, BUT I'VE PAID YOU FOR PASSAGE!
IT'S GONNA COST YOU SOME MORE FOR THAT WOMAN'S CABIN! KIDNAPPING RUNS HIGH ON THIS SHIP!
WHILE THIS IS GOING ON, A SMALL BUNDLE SAILS OUT OF A PORTHOLE ONTO THE DOCKS – JUST AS THE SHIP GETS UNDER WAY...
MILTON CANIFF

7/15
Copyright 1955, Field Enterprises, Inc. Registered U.S. Patent Office.
WELL, HONEY, WE'RE UNDER WAY... AND NOW YOU REALLY ARE HELPLESS...
YOU'RE CUT OFF FROM SHORE —AND STEVE CANYON WILL BE THE BIGGEST BOOB ON FORMOSA!
THIS IS THE PERFECT CAT-AND-MOUSE GAME! —I LIKE TO ENJOY THE SUSPENSE—WHEN I KNOW I'M GOING TO WIN!
MEANWHILE = ON THE BRIDGE
CHOW IS DOWN, SKIPPER! COME AND GET IT, OR I'LL THROW IT IN THE SCUPPERS
HUH? WHO ARE YOU?
MILTON CANIFF
SMELL THIS AND YOU WON'T CARE!.. I'M JUST A GOOD SHIP'S COOK WHO LIKES DOING THAT BETTER THAN BEING A MARINE!
A DESERTER, HUH?—WELL, I'LL EAT THE STUFF—THEN DECIDE WHETHER I'LL FIND YOU STOWED AWAY NOW—OR AT THE END OF OUR RUN...

7/16
Copyright 1955, Field Enterprises, Inc. Registered U.S. Patent Office.
KID, YOU CAN COOK! —THAT MEAT MANGLER NOW IN THE GALLEY'LL BE YOUR ASSISTANT TILL THE END OF THE RUN —WHEN I 'DISCOVER' I HAVE A MARINE DESERTER ABOARD!
THANKS, SKIPPER! —NOW I CAN LET THE OLD COOK OUT OF THE FREEZER!
SO REED KIMBERLY HAS INGRATIATED HIMSELF ABOARD THE SHIP ON WHICH HIMMERSKORN IS HOLDING MRS. HALL...
MILTON CANIFF
...WHILE ON THE DOCKS STEVE CANYON AND THE SHORE PATROL SEARCH FOR THE MISSING WOMAN... AS THEY MOVE TOWARD A STRANGE LITTLE BUNDLE LYING IN THEIR PATH...

STEVE CANYON
by MILTON CANIFF
WHAT HAVE YOU GOT, CAR 12? OVER...
THIS IS CAR 12 ON THE CONSULATE STAKEOUT... P.F.C. KIMBERLY HAS NOT ATTEMPTED TO CONTACT THE HALL GIRL, MRS. HALL IS STILL MISSING FROM THE HOUSE...
SHORE PATROL
U.S. NAVY
U.S. NAVY
MEANWHILE = ON BOARD A TRAMP COASTAL VESSEL OFF FORMOSA...
BABY, IT'S REAL COMICAL, YOU AND THAT FLYBOY CANYON THINKING YOU COULD OUT-ANGLE OL' ROY HIMMERSKORN...
CANYON AND HIS STOOGES ARE PROBABLY STILL FOLLOWING THE DECOY-SET UP!
THE CAPTAIN OF THIS TUB AND I HAVE A NICE LITTLE WORKING ARRANGEMENT...
BUT WHERE DOES THAT PUT YOU AND ME, BABY?
...YOU'VE BLASTED MY PLANS FOR A CORNER ON BLACK MARKET POLIO VACCINE IN FORMOSA — AND I SHOULD GET RID OF YOU FAST AND EASY...
BUT I AM STILL FASCINATED BY A BEAUTIFUL BLIND WOMAN...

YOU'RE SO COMPLETELY HELPLESS!.. I CAN HOLD ONE HAND AND YOU CAN'T EVEN SEE ME TO HIT ME WITH THE OTHER!
I CAN HOLD YOU SO YOU CAN'T MOVE, AND KISS YOU AS OFT--
KNOCK KNOCK
WHAT IN BLAZES DO YOU WANT?
I'M YOUR STEWARD, SIR! YES, SIR—I HAVE DINNER FOR YOU AND MADAME, SIR!
I'M THE KIND OF STEWARD YOU READ ABOUT! I'M A LIVIN' JEWEL! A ROUGH DIAMOND!—IF YOU KNOW WHAT I MEAN...
MEANWHILE... STEVE AND THE SHORE PATROL SEARCH THE DOCKS FOR A CLUE
OUR REPORTS NARROW IT DOWN!—THEY MUST HAVE LEFT FORMOSA BY BOAT!
NO SCOOP FROM THE LOCAL JUNK CAPTAINS... NOT THAT THEY WOULD TELL YOU ANYTHING...
SAY, COLONEL CANYON, THIS IS AN ODD THING!—A BATCH OF KNITTING! IT WAS BACK IN THE CORNER...
IT'S HERS! GILBERTA HALL'S!.. BUT LOOK WHAT SHE'S DONE!!
Copyright 1955, Field Enterprises, Inc.
7-17

7/18
BUT COL. CANYON, IT'S JUST A PIECE OF KNITTING AND SOME YARN...
IT'S GILBERTA HALL'S KNITTING! I REMEMBER THE SCARF SHE WAS WORKING ON! —NOW LOOK AT THE LAST ROW!
MILTON CANIFF
Copyright 1955, Field Enterprises, Inc. Registered U.S. Patent Office.
KIND OF AN UNEVEN STRING OF PURLING AND KNITTING...
READ IT AS DOTS AND DASHES! IT SAYS "S.S. GONQUIN"!
MUST BE THE BOAT SHE IS ON! THE 7th FLEET DESTROYER PATROL CAN RUN IT DOWN!
SHE MIGHT BE KILLED IF A DESTROYER CLOSED IN—BUT THERE'S ANOTHER WAY...
WHILE ON THE SHIP
WELL—I GUESS I CAN EAT, AT THAT! —PUT IT DOWN, STEWARD!
LET ME SERVE IT, SIR! I MOVE SWIFTLY—AS A REED IN THE WIND!

7/19
...AND SO WE THINK MRS. HALL IS HELD ON BOARD THE TRAMP STEAMER 'GONQUIN'... OVER...
ROGER, CANYON! WE'LL MAKE A RADIO CHECK ON SHIPS IN THE PATROL ZONE IN ALPHABETICAL ORDER! THE 'GONQUIN' WON'T RISK SILENCE, MORE ESPECIALLY IF SHE IS CARRYING MRS. HALL!
MILTON CANIFF
Copyright 1955, Field Enterprises, Inc. Registered U.S. Patent Office.
WHILE ON BOARD THE 'GONQUIN'...
YOU DID NOT EAT, MRS. HALL, HONEY
BUT I HAVE DINED WELL—AND NOW I CAN GIVE YOU MY FULL ATTENTION...
YOU'LL BE GLAD YOU FLUBBED YOUR TRY AT INCRIMINATING ME... I AM A MUCH MORE EXCITING PERSON THAN ANY HIDEBOUND DIPLOMAT HUSB---
YESSIREE! HERE I COME TO REMOVE THE DISHES! A BUSBOY AS FAITHFUL AS OLD DOG TRAY! HAHAHA!

7/20
Copyright 1955, Field Enterprises, Inc. Registered U. S. Patent Office.
GET OUT!
SURE! SURE! JUST TRYING TO EARN MY TIP, MISTER!
BEAT IT!
OKAY! OKAY!
NOW, BABY— I--
KNOCK! KNOCK!
MILTON CANIFF
WHAT TH--
SIR, I JUST WANTED TO TELL YOU THE TIP COULD WAIT TILL THE END OF THE TRIP!

7/21
Copyright 1955, Field Enterprises, Inc. Registered U. S. Patent Office.
I'LL TAKE OFF YOUR GLASSES, BABY...YOU WON'T WANT THEM WHEN YOU'RE KISSING ME!
BY THE WAY—I NEVER DID TELL YOU WHAT I LOOK LIKE...
YOU HAVEN'T SEEN ANY OF THE CURRENT MOVIE ACTORS, BUT I'M SORTA THE VALENTINO TYPE... WITH A CREW CUT...
DON'T TRY TO STRUGGLE, HONEY...
THERE'S NO WAY YOU CAN HURT ME-EE!
MILTON CANIFF

7/22
Copyright 1955, Field Enterprises, Inc. Registered U. S. Patent Office.
COL. CANYON, WE GOT A FIX ON S.S. 'GONQUIN'! HERE'S THE SCOOP!
LET'S GO! BUT DON'T ALARM THE 'GONQUIN'S' CREW! WE WANT TO FIND MRS. HALL ALIVE!
MEANWHILE
I'LL CLOSE THE WINDOW SO THAT CRAZY STEWARD CAN'T DISTURB US AGAIN, HONEY! THEN---
HEY! SMOKE!
MILTON CANIFF
FIRE! HELP!
OH, SO SORRY, SIR—MUSTA GOT THE GALLEY STOVEPIPE STUCK INTO THE VENTILATOR SYSTEM! I GUESS MAYBE THAT KNOCKS THE BIG TIP YOU WERE GOING TO GIVE ME, DOESN'T IT?

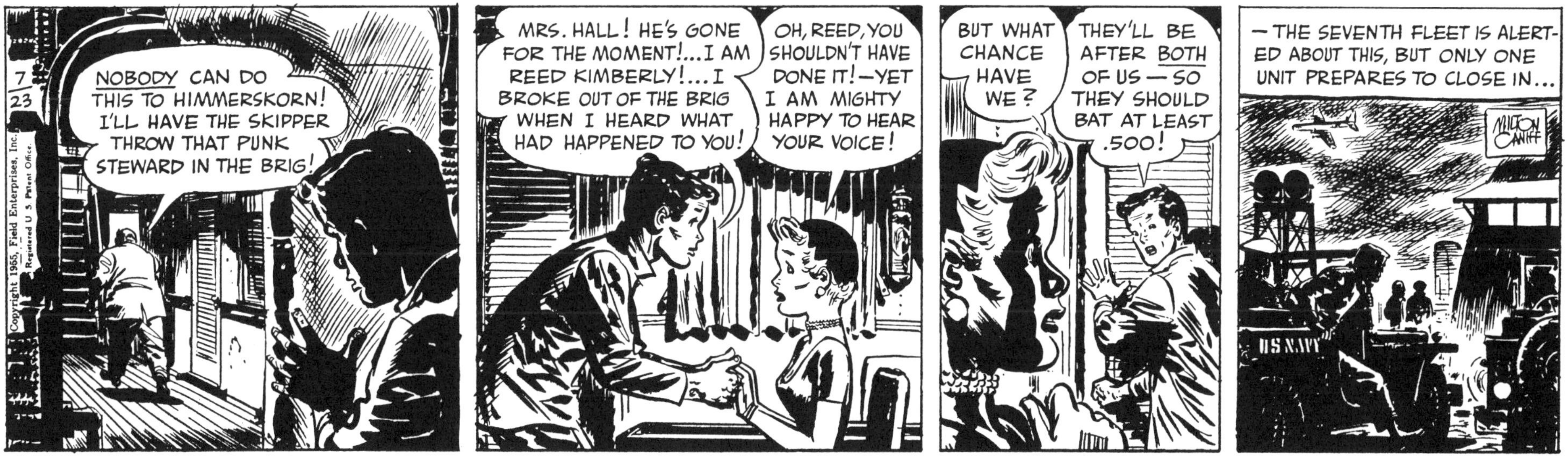
7/23
Copyright 1955, Field Enterprises, Inc. Registered U. S. Patent Office.
NOBODY CAN DO THIS TO HIMMERSKORN! I'LL HAVE THE SKIPPER THROW THAT PUNK STEWARD IN THE BRIG!
MRS. HALL! HE'S GONE FOR THE MOMENT!... I AM REED KIMBERLY!... I BROKE OUT OF THE BRIG WHEN I HEARD WHAT HAD HAPPENED TO YOU!
OH, REED, YOU SHOULDN'T HAVE DONE IT!—YET I AM MIGHTY HAPPY TO HEAR YOUR VOICE!
BUT WHAT CHANCE HAVE WE?
THEY'LL BE AFTER BOTH OF US — SO THEY SHOULD BAT AT LEAST .500!
— THE SEVENTH FLEET IS ALERTED ABOUT THIS, BUT ONLY ONE UNIT PREPARES TO CLOSE IN...
MILTON CANIFF
US NAVY

STEVE CANYON
by MILTON CANIFF
WE ASSUME MRS. HALL IS ON BOARD THE TRAMP STEAMER "S.S. GONQUIN"
SHE STITCHED THAT NAME IN MORSE CODE INTO THE SCARF SHE WAS KNITTING!..WE FOUND THE BUNDLE ON THE DOCK...
U.S. NAVY
WE SPOTTED THE S.S. GONQUIN'S PRESENT POSITION BY A RADIO CHECK...
SO WE HAVE SOME PLANS! —FIRST WE'LL--
MEANWHILE= ON BOARD THE GONQUIN...
CAPTAIN, YOU'VE GOT TO PUT THAT STEWARD IN CHAINS! I--
A STOWAWAY WHO CAN COOK LIKE THAT?... DON'T MAKE ME LAUGH, HIMMER-SKORN...
YOU FOULED THE POLIO VACCINE DEAL YOU CLAIMED YOU HAD RIGGED IN FOR-MOSA... OUR BARGAIN WAS THAT I'D GET YOU AWAY! NOW SHOVE OFF! MY CHOW IS ABOUT DUE!

MRS. HALL, THIS IS THE FIRST TIME I'VE HAD A CHANCE TO REALLY TALK TO YOU... DON'T GIVE UP — WE'LL PULL OUT OF THIS...
BUT, REED, HONEY, HOW IN THE WORLD DID YOU GET FROM THE NAVY BRIG TO THIS BOAT?
SO THAT'S IT! YOU KNOW THIS PUNK!
YES, SHE KNOWS ME — AND YOU SHOULD, TOO! YOU PLANTED THE POLIO VACCINE IN MY CAP IN THE BLUE CAT CAFÉ...
LISTEN! I HEAR AN ENGINE!
YEE-OW! IT'S A--
THE MARINE WILL KEEP IN THE CABIN CLOSET FOR A WHILE...
BUT, BABY, I'LL HAVE TO GET RID OF YOU! — AND THERE'S JUST ONE PLACE THEY WON'T LOOK!
...AND AFTER YOU HANG DOWN IN THOSE FUEL OIL FUMES INSIDE THE FUNNEL FOR A LITTLE WHILE YOU'RE NOT GOING TO BE TELLING ANY TALES, EITHER...
Copyright 1955, Field Enterprises, Inc.
7-24

7/25
Copyright 1955, Field Enterprises, Inc. Registered U.S. Patent Office.
REED KIMBERLY COMES TO HIS SENSES INSIDE THE CLOSET OF HIMMERSKORN'S CABIN—THERE IS THE SOUND OF RUNNING FEET ON THE DECK...
HE MUSTA SLUGGED ME...
MEANWHILE = HIMMERSKORN IS CLIMBING THE GONQUIN'S FUNNEL, CARRYING MRS. HALL OVER HIS SHOULDER...
PATROL BOATS MUST BE CLOSE – I CAN HEAR THEIR ENGINES
THEY WON'T THINK OF LOOKING FOR MRS. HALL HANGING BY HER FEET INSIDE THE STACK...
AND THE OIL FUMES WILL QUIET HER IN A HURRY!
...BUT AT THIS MOMENT THE 'BOATS' HIMMERSKORN HEARD RISE FROM WATER LEVEL TO MAST HEIGHT— AND THE SHIP IS BATHED IN LIGHT FROM HELICOPTERS!
MILTON CANIFF

7/26
Copyright 1955, Field Enterprises, Inc. Registered U.S. Patent Office.
AHOY, THE BRIDGE!
BRING YOUR VESSEL INTO THE WIND AND KEEP HER SO! MAINTAIN STEERAGE WAY ONLY!
MILTON CANIFF
I KNEW THOSE RADIO POSITION CHECKS MEANT TROUBLE!
I'LL GO PUT HIMMERSKORN AND THE WOMAN IN IRONS BEFORE THE FEDERALS COME ABOARD!
LOOK, SIR! WHAT'S GOING ON TOPSIDE THE GONQUIN'S FUNNEL?
...A MAN LETTING SOMEBODY DOWN INTO IT!— NAYLOR! BREAK OUT OXYGEN GEAR! WE'LL WINCH YOU DOWN AND COVER YOU! STOP THAT MURDER!
AYE, AYE, SIR!
NAVY
12

7/27
Copyright 1955, Field Enterprises, Inc. Registered U. S. Patent Office.
HEY! SOMEONE IN THE CLOSET!
I'LL PUT HIMMERSKORN AND THE WOMAN IN IRONS AND TELL THE NAVY I WAS HOLDING THEM TO BE PICKED UP...
THE CAPTAIN UNLOCKS THE DOOR, AND REED KIMBERLY SLAMS HIS WAY OUT...
...JUST IN TIME TO SEE HIMMERSKORN CLIMB DOWN THE GONQUIN'S FUNNEL ... LEAVING MRS. HALL DANGLING AMID THE OIL FUMES INSIDE ...
MILTON CANIFF

7/28
Copyright 1955, Field Enterprises, Inc. Registered U. S. Patent Office
WEARING AN OXYGEN MASK, A SAILOR FROM THE HOVERING HELICOPTER LIFTS MRS. HALL OUT OF THE GONQUIN'S FUNNEL ... THEN LOWERS HER TO THE STEAMER'S DECK ...
MEANWHILE=STEVE CANYON AND MEN FROM THE OTHER RESCUE HELICOPTER HAVE LANDED ...
...WHILE HIMMERSKORN RUNS FROM THE FUNNEL
MILTON CANIFF

7/29
Copyright 1955, Field Enterprises, Inc
Registered U S Patent Office
WAIT, NOW, STEWARD— I DIDN'T MEAN...
I'M NOT A STEWARD! I CAME TO PAY YOU BACK FOR SLIPPING POLIO SERUM INTO MY CAP...
MILTON CANIFF
I HAVE SOME GOOD STOUT ROPE—AND WHERE YOU ARE WILL PASS FOR THE YARD-ARM!

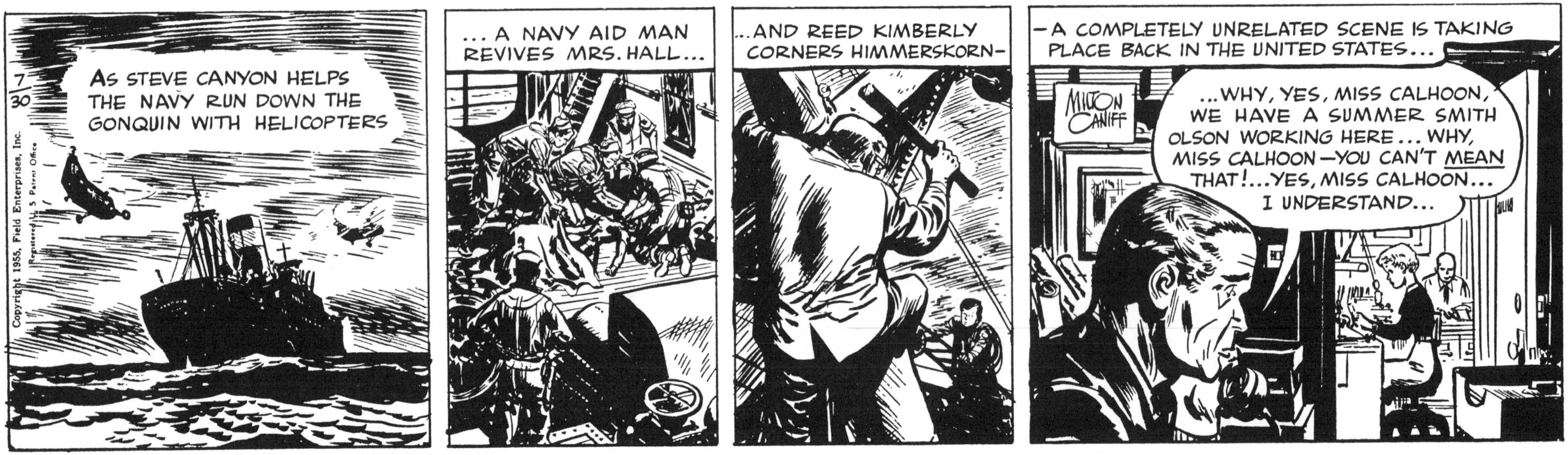
7/30
Copyright 1955, Field Enterprises, Inc.
Registered U S Patent Office
AS STEVE CANYON HELPS THE NAVY RUN DOWN THE GONQUIN WITH HELICOPTERS
... A NAVY AID MAN REVIVES MRS. HALL...
...AND REED KIMBERLY CORNERS HIMMERSKORN—
—A COMPLETELY UNRELATED SCENE IS TAKING PLACE BACK IN THE UNITED STATES...
MILTON CANIFF
...WHY, YES, MISS CALHOON, WE HAVE A SUMMER SMITH OLSON WORKING HERE... WHY, MISS CALHOON—YOU CAN'T MEAN THAT!...YES, MISS CALHOON... I UNDERSTAND...

STEVE CANYON
by MILTON CANIFF
GET MORE OXYGEN FROM THE HELICOPTER! MRS. HALL HAD A ROUGH DOSE OF OIL FUMES, BUT SHE'S COMING AROUND!
...JAKE USED IT FULL STRENGTH WHEN WE LET HIM DOWN FROM THE CHOPPER TO PULL HER OUT OF THE FUNNEL...
WHERE'S REED KIMBERLY ?
HE TOOK OFF AFTER HIMMERSKORN, SIR!
GO AWAY! I-I'LL H-HIT YOU! YOU'LL FALL!
REED! COME DOWN FROM THERE! WE'LL STARVE HIMMERSKORN OFF HIS PERCH!
I CAN'T HEAR YOU, COL. CANYON, SIR— ON ACCOUNT OF THIS GUY MOANIN' AND GROANIN'!
MAYBE HE'S SCARED!...

THE WAY I WAS WHEN THEY GRABBED ME FOR THE POLIO VACCINE HE STOWED IN MY CAP!...
...OR THE WAY MRS. HALL WAS WHEN HE DRAGGED HER ON BOARD THIS BUCKET...
IF I'M TO BE COURT-MARTIALED, IT MIGHT AS WELL BE FOR SOMETHING BIG!.. SO I'M COMING AFTER YOU
PRIVATE KIMBERLY REPORTING IN ARREST, SIR!
MEANWHILE = A LONG WAY FROM FORMOSA...
I'M SORRY, MRS. OLSON, BUT I HAVE NO CHOICE... I MUST LET YOU GO!
Copyright 1955, Field Enterprises, Inc.
7-31

8/1
OOOHH
WHAT HAPPENED?
WELL, HIMMERSKORN, MAYBE YOU WEREN'T SO LUCKY! —REED KIMBERLY GOT A LINE AROUND YOUR ANKLE BEFORE YOU FLOPPED OFF THE MAST...
COL. CANYON, SIR, I SAID I AM REPORTING TO YOU IN ARREST!
OKAY, REED —RELAX!.. YOU'LL HAVE PLENTY OF TIME TO STAND AT ATTENTION
HOW IS MRS. HALL?
SIR, SHE TOOK A BLAST OF THOSE FUMES, BUT SHE'S HEADING NORTH
MILTON CANIFF
GIL, IT'S STEVE CANYON! —I'M SORRY I GOT YOU INTO ALL THIS!
HUSH, STEVE...DON'T STOP MY THINKING I'M A HEROINE...IT KEEPS ME FROM VISUALIZING WHAT A MESS I MUST BE!

8/2
STEVE, MAY I SPEAK TO REED KIMBERLY?
MADAME HALL, YOU MAY HAVE THE KEYS TO THE CITY—AFTER WHAT YOU'VE BEEN THROUGH!
REED, HONEY, I HEAR YOU BROKE OUT OF THE BRIG TO HELP ME PROTECT HOLLY...
WELL, MA'AM, IT'S HOW I FEEL ABOUT HOLLY...
MAYBE I HAVE NO RIGHT TO BE IN LOVE WITH HER, BUT I JUST AM!...DO YOU KNOW WHAT I MEAN, MRS. HALL?
Y-YES—I CAN UNDERSTAND THAT FEELING...
MILTON CANIFF

8/3
Copyright 1953, Field Enterprises, Inc. Registered U. S. Patent Office
STEVE, WHERE IS REED KIMBERLY ?
HE AND HIMMER-SKORN ARE UNDER GUARD IN THE OTHER HELICOPTER, GIL... WE LEFT A 'PRIZE' CREW ON BOARD THE GONQUIN!
MILTON CANIFF
WE RADIOED AHEAD SO THE NAVY COULD BRING HOLLY OUT TO MEET YOU...
ENSIGN, I DON'T SEE MISS HALL! DIDN'T YOU RECEIVE OUR MESSAGE TO BRING HER HERE ?
OH, YES, SIR, COL. CANYON...
NAVY
...BUT SHE WENT TO THE OTHER HELICOPTER TO SEE PRIVATE KIMBERLY...

8/4
Copyright 1953, Field Enterprises, Inc. Registered U. S. Patent Office
OH, HELLO, COLONEL CANYON!
YOUR MOTHER WAS IN THE OTHER HELICOPTER, HOLLY! I'LL GIVE YOU A LIFT OVER THERE!
U.S. NAVY
QUITE A NATURAL MISTAKE FOR YOU TO GO TO THE WRONG AIRCRAFT, HOLLY, BUT IT MIGHT SEEM STRANGE TO YOUR MOTHER...
COL. CANYON, SIR, Y'ALL DECIDED TO GO INTRIGUIN' AN' CONNIVIN' WITHOUT TELLIN' ME, SO I RECKON Y'ALL DIDN'T NEED ME TO GREET YOU...
U.S. NAVY
LISTEN, HOLLY!. YOUR MOTHER GOT INTO THIS TO TRAP HIMMERSKORN AS THE PERSON WHO SLIPPED THE POLIO VACCINE INTO REED'S CAP! SHE DID IT SO YOUR NAME WOULDN'T TURN UP IN A NATIVE BLACK MARKET STORY — AND SHE HAS SUCCEEDED!
DON'T YOU LECTURE ME LIKE A DRILL SERGEANT, STEVE CANYON! DON'T YOU THINK I KNOW YOU'RE TRYIN' TO TAKE MY MOTHER AWAY FROM MY DADDY ?
MILTON CANIFF

8/5
Copyright 1955, Field Enterprises, Inc. Registered U.S. Patent Office.
HOLD THE PHONE!
WHAT'S THIS ABOUT ME TRYING TO TAKE YOUR MOTHER AWAY FROM YOUR DAD?
OH, STEVE CANYON, YOU THINK I'M SUCH A CHILD... I DECLARE, I'LL BET EVERY LIVIN' SOUL ON THIS POST—EXCEPT MY DADDY—THINKS YOU AN' MY MOTHER ARE IN LOVE!
NOW, IF YOU'LL DRIVE ME ON OVER I'LL GREET MY POOR BLIND DARLIN' AS I SHOULD!
MEANWHILE = BACK IN THE UNITED STATES...
...THIS IS 27! SUMMER OLSON WENT TO THE EMPLOYMENT OFFICE OF A FACTORY HERE... SHE DIDN'T COME OUT SO I SENT HER A WIRE — WHICH CAME BACK UNDELIVERED, 'ADDRESEE UNKNOWN'— SO SHE MUSTA USED A FAKE NAME...
MILTON CANIFF

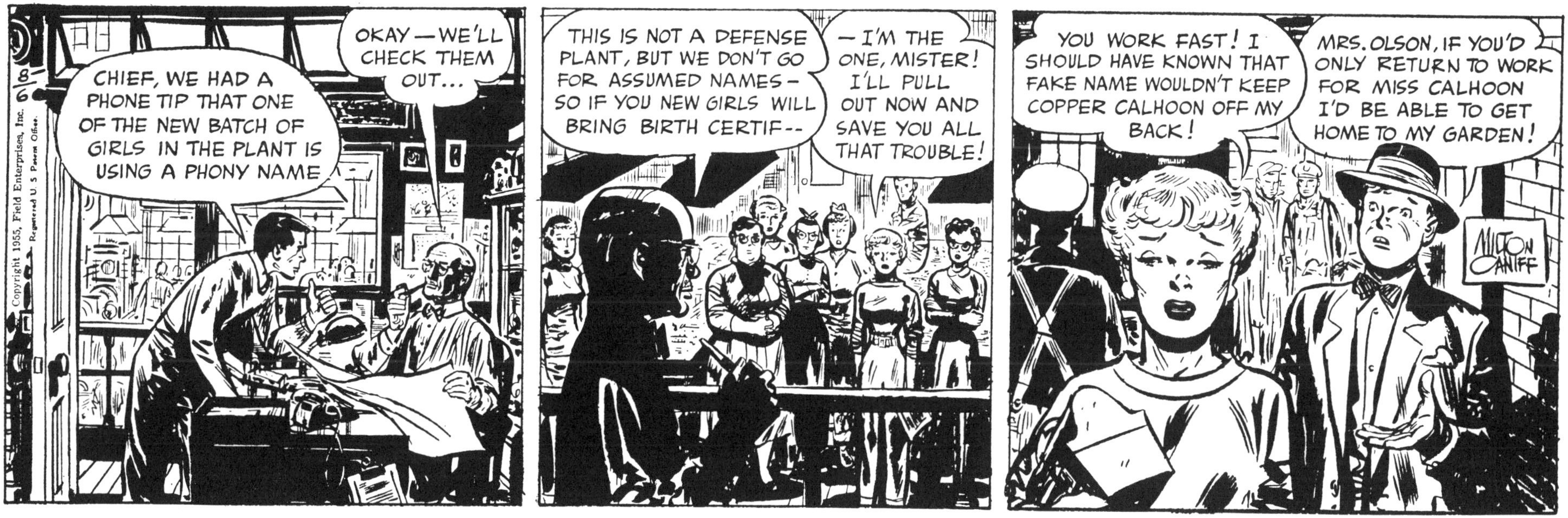
8/6
Copyright 1955, Field Enterprises, Inc. Registered U.S. Patent Office.
CHIEF, WE HAD A PHONE TIP THAT ONE OF THE NEW BATCH OF GIRLS IN THE PLANT IS USING A PHONY NAME
OKAY—WE'LL CHECK THEM OUT...
THIS IS NOT A DEFENSE PLANT, BUT WE DON'T GO FOR ASSUMED NAMES—SO IF YOU NEW GIRLS WILL BRING BIRTH CERTIF--
—I'M THE ONE, MISTER! I'LL PULL OUT NOW AND SAVE YOU ALL THAT TROUBLE!
YOU WORK FAST! I SHOULD HAVE KNOWN THAT FAKE NAME WOULDN'T KEEP COPPER CALHOON OFF MY BACK!
MRS. OLSON, IF YOU'D ONLY RETURN TO WORK FOR MISS CALHOON I'D BE ABLE TO GET HOME TO MY GARDEN!
MILTON CANIFF

STEVE CANYON
by MILTON CANIFF
GIL, I HAVEN'T FORGIVEN MYSELF FOR ALLOWING YOU TO GET MIXED UP IN THE HIMMER-SKORN CASE...
WHY, STEVE CANYON— HOW YOU DO TAKE ON...
I DECLARE, YOU SEEM TO FORGET THAT I ACCOMPLISHED MY PURPOSE!... MY DARLING DAUGHTER'S NAME WAS NEVER MENTIONED IN CONNECTION WITH THE BLACK MARKET IN POLIO VACCINE!
REED KIMBERLY WILL BE DOING EXTRA DUTY UNTIL THE MARINE CORPS RUNS OUT OF ASSIGNMENTS
HIMMERSKORN WON'T BE IN-VESTING IN FORMOSAN INDUSTRY...
SO MUCH FOR THAT! I MUST GET INTO THE AIR AND EARN MY FLIGHT PAY..
WELL, YOU HURRY BACK NOW, Y'HEAR?

WHEN YOU'RE RELAXED, YOUR SPEECH IS MORE SOUTHERN...'BYE
HE THINKS I'M RELAXED! MAYBE HE IS MORE BLIND THAN I!
MEANWHILE = BACK IN THE STATES
YOU'RE HERE TOO ?
HIYA, MRS. OLSON...
AS SOON AS I GET A JOB, YOU SHOW UP!.. HAVEN'T YOU GOT A CONSCIENCE?
I DON'T DO ANYTHING TO YOU, LADY...
NO—YOU MERELY FOLLOW ME AROUND!..WHEN I START TO WORK, YOU NOTIFY COPPER CALHOON, AND SHE PUTS PRESSURE ON MY NEW EMPLOYER UNTIL I AM FIRED...
IT'S NOTHIN' PERSONAL AGAINST YOU, MA'AM —I GOTTA KEEP MY JOB, Y'KNOW!
TELL MISS CALHOON THAT I AM TAKING A CIVIL SERVICE EXAMINATION — I DON'T THINK SHE CAN THREATEN TO CANCEL HER COMPANY'S ORDERS FROM THE UNITED STATES GOVERNMENT!
I ADMIRE YOUR SPUNK, MA'AM!..I'LL PUT WHAT YOU SAID RIGHT IN MY REGULAR REPORT!
Copyright 1955, Field Enterprises, Inc.
8-7

8/8
Copyright 1955, Field Enterprises, Inc.
Registered U.S. Patent Office
HELLO, NAMU, THIS IS COL. CANYON SPEAKING.
HOW ARE MRS. HALL AND MISS HOLLY?
OKAY, FINE, I GUESS SO, SOR...
WHAT DO YOU MEAN YOU 'GUESS SO'? MAYBE I'D BETTER SPEAK TO MRS. HALL!
MIZZY HALL SHE WRITE OUT WHAT NAMU TO SAY TO COL. CANYONS..." I HAVE TAKING MOTHER TO VISIT FRIENDS —WHERE SHE BE SAFE FROM ALL KINDS DANGERS-
"...INCLUDING CERTAIN BLOND AIR FORCE LOO-TENT COLONELS WHO SHALL BE NAMELESS..."
MILTON CANIFF